MW00830901

BOUND BY BLOOD

A COZY FANTASY ROMANCE WITH HEARTY SOUP, AN UGLY PUP, A CURSED BLOOD FAE, AND A LONELY HUMAN

STARRY KINGDOMS OF THE FAE

JESSICA M. BUTLER

Jessica M Butler

Copyright © 2023 by Jessica M. Butler.

All rights reserved.

No part of this book may be reproduced in any form or by any electronic or mechanical means, including information storage and retrieval systems, without written permission from the author, except for the use of brief quotations in a book review.

Jessica M. Butler/Enchanting Chimera Publishing

Publisher's Note: This is a work of fiction. Names, characters, places, and incidents are a product of the author's imagination. Locales and public names are sometimes used for atmospheric purposes. Any resemblance to actual people, living or dead, or to businesses, companies, events, institutions, or locales is completely coincidental.

Cover Art by Franziska Stern @coverdungeonrabbit

www.coverdungeon.com

Underjacket Art by Natálie Vašutová @Thalia_Art

www.jmbutlerauthor.com

Send feedback or concerns for the book to

jessicambutlerauthor@gmail.com

Instagram: jessicambutlerauthor

First Edition

Printed in the United States of America

CONTENTS

Dedicated with great love and affection to all those who know love at first sight is 100% possible and practically guaranteed when one sees puppies, kittens, bunnies, and the like.

STRANGE VISITORS IN THE NIGHT

It wasn't wise to go out alone at night, but that didn't keep Erryn from sleeping with her windows open in late summer. Being a soup maker had many perks. Especially in winter. But in the summer? She leaned against the windowsill and took in a deep breath. Lots of good food was a fantastic perk. The heat that came with it was not so pleasant this time of year.

Polph, she hated the humidity. It made her hair go wild in the worst way possible, and she felt constantly sticky. That awkward temperature between soothing warmth and annoying heat with far too much damp to be pleasant for anyone. Except maybe frogs and salamanders.

Thank goodness it was almost autumn. This unusual hot spell was supposed to end tomorrow or a couple days after in a series of chilling storms.

Huffing, she rested her chin onto her palm and

stared out into the moon-drenched landscape. It wouldn't come soon enough.

The heavy clouds hadn't obscured the moon yet. Barely even a breath of wind stirred the leaves of the hickory tree just outside her window, let alone in the dark forest beyond the boundary marker and in the Barrens Wild. It had to be stifling in there tonight. At least she had her open windows and the cross breeze. If the wind ever started to blow again.

Polph. Was the night going to last forever? Not that she should be complaining.

She blew a raspberry against her wrist and then shook her head. No point in even trying to sleep. She had half a mind to strip off her thin white cotton shift and sleep in the nude.

But then she'd have to close the windows.

No. She just needed to occupy her mind until the sleepiness returned.

Her lute leaned against the wall beneath the window where she'd left it the last time she'd played. One of the only things left from her old life. It fit perfectly against her, though, and her fingers swiftly found their place as she leaned back against the window frame.

No song in particular rose to her mind. She just let her fingers wander over the strings, a melody of some sort forming through the meandering. Once she'd believed that her ability to play and dance and sing all at once would be the key to her great fortune and the answer to her destiny. Now, though...well, it was comfort on a hot night and solace against the silence when what she really wanted was someone to talk to.

People like her didn't get family again. They didn't deserve it. Some mistakes could never be undone.

She stared.

It was wrong. No question about it. What she had done was selfish and horrid. And there was nothing she could do to fix it. Nothing to do to turn back what had happened.

She sighed, closing her eyes as she tried to push those intrusive thoughts away.

Something splashed in the creek.

Scowling, she stopped playing and turned toward the sound. What could that be?

Rapid footsteps followed, the splashing increasing. It sounded like a smaller creature running.

A strong impulse to open the door and go out to see struck her.

It wasn't safe. Of course it wasn't.

Except not everything in the night was evil. And lately, the nights had been stiller.

Small whimpering cries followed.

She peered around the corner as best she could, squinting. Everyone had warned her against talking to strange things in the dark, but what was the point of wards and charms if you had to be suspicious all the time? In all her travels, she'd never known it to go that badly.

"Hello?" she called out. Her voice sounded weak and small in the night. Almost tinny.

The whimpering cry intensified along with the

splashes. Then a soft patter of footsteps raced up to the house.

She blinked.

Beneath the window scratched a small winged dog, dark-brown and black scaled with irregular tufts of fur and bright red eyes. It looked like some sort of pug and bulldog mixture with a tiny stub of a tail. Its soft little cry cut straight through her heart. It might be the ugliest thing she'd ever seen, but clearly the poor darling was terrified.

"Oh, baby," she whispered. "What's wrong?"

What even was it? Was it a dog or a dragon or something else?

It glanced back over its shoulder. Its ears laid flat down the back of its skull as it howled and scratched faster at the wall, jumping up.

"Are you in trouble?" She started to lean out but remembered the warnings.

No. She was human. She shouldn't go out beyond the boundaries of the house. But maybe…

She gestured toward the door. "Come on, baby."

The dog let loose another howl, then stopped short.

She hurried from her bedroom to the kitchen with its small sitting area and broad door. It only took a few seconds to unfasten the heavy black iron bolts over the door.

Little claws scraped at the door, the cries intensifying. As she flung the door open, the odd little creature peered up at her. It whined, lifting one tiny dark paw as if asking for permission.

She glanced out once more.

The wards would protect her from anything malicious that might change its form to gain entrance.

Crouching down, she held out her hand. "Come on, sweetheart. It's all right."

The dog inched forward, its dark wings folded tightly across its back. Poor darling was so ugly and yet adorable all at once. The uneven tufts of fur made it look a touch ragged, but hope shone in those big red eyes. That little stub of a tail wagged faster as it sniffed her fingertips, then gave her a tentative lick. The reptilian wings reminded her of little dragon wings. Was it a dog-dragon? Was there such a thing? It had tiny little tusks protruding from its mouth.

"Yes, it's all right," she said. "Come on."

It came closer, continuing to sniff and lick at her fingers as its tail wagged so fast it shook the whole of its hindquarters.

If ever there was a little creature in need of a home, it was this one. It had no collar or markings to indicate where it belonged. Looked like a male. He whimpered as she scratched behind his ear.

"Are you thirsty, sweetheart?"

She started to stand, then froze. Footsteps splashed through the creek, drawing rapidly nearer.

Her heart clenched. She had been paying so much attention to the dog that she had forgotten about the door.

The dog twisted around as well, giving a yip of alarm.

As she moved toward the door, a dark figure raced

up toward the house. "Get back here!" an angry male voice shouted.

Rustling garments and heavy footsteps drew closer. The dog barked and ran behind her legs.

She straightened as she saw the stranger. Oh, thank all that was good this house was warded and consecrated because that was a blood fae.

He was easily several inches taller than she with a strong frame highlighted by the dark-blue velvet garb he wore. He might have been handsome except his expression was contorted with fury as he glared down at the little dog.

"Don't shout at him," she snapped, scooping the dog up.

The poor creature clearly wanted nothing to do with the fae. And while it really wasn't smart to shout at a blood fae, she was safe in her home. For now. He couldn't cross the threshold or enter unless she invited him. And—well—an odd protectiveness for this little creature had come over her. If anything happened to him, she would die.

"Can't you see he's scared?"

"He?" The fae straightened, seeming to notice her for the first time. A bewildered expression pinched his face. His deep-purple eyes narrowed. "That's not a real anything, human. That's a magical apparition that took the wrong shape, and it has gotten out of hand. Return it to me now. It does not belong to you."

"What are you going to do with him?"

How had this fae gotten past the wards anyway? What magic did he really have?

He shook his head at her, his lip curling. "I don't owe you answers. What I do with my magic is my own business."

"He's in my house. That makes this my business. I don't let anyone hurt dogs."

"That's not a dog!" He stalked closer but halted at the threshold. "Hand that over. The longer this takes, the worse it gets."

"What do you mean 'worse?'" she demanded, stepping back farther into the house. "What are you going to do with him?"

"It's none of your concern what I do with my magic. Turn that thing over now!" His gaze darkened.

"No!" She returned the glare.

"So be it." He twisted his hand around as if seizing something from the air.

The dog yipped, his eyes bugging as he started to levitate in the air out of her arms and toward the door.

No!

She swept her arms up and caught hold of the ugly pup. His wings folded tight to his back as he cowered against her.

"You let this dog go right now!" Hugging him to her chest, she resisted the tug and pull. How was that even working? The wards were supposed to prevent that. "Let him go *now!*"

The blood fae's eyes widened. He dropped his hand to his side. "That isn't yours. You can't do that. You're supposed to let go."

"You aren't welcome here!" She slammed the door in his face.

Stupid blood fae.

"I beg your pardon!" he shouted from the other side.

"Beg all you like, it doesn't change that you aren't welcome." She scratched the little dog under the chin. He barely weighed anything at all. "Poor darling. Was the bad fae trying to hurt you?"

This really was bad. She needed to figure out some way to diffuse the situation. Fae held grudges, and while she was safe in here, that wasn't a permanent thing.

"You can't hide in there forever. That's my magic you're holding. I need it back now. How dare you steal from a blood fae!"

She snuggled the dog closer. He whimpered as he curled up against her. "Don't worry, sweetheart," she whispered. "I won't let him anywhere near you." She then glared at the door as if he could see her through it. "Listen up, fancy fae man, I am not impressed, and I won't let you near this dog."

"Fancy fae man?" Indignation filled the fae's voice, sending it into a higher octave. He almost sounded like a boy for a moment. "I am of a legendary family, one of great renown."

"Really? Renowned for what? Bad taste?"

Creator preserve her, she just couldn't keep her mouth shut. Antagonizing a blood fae worked as well as adding old onions, wrinkled jalapenos, and aged habaneros to the stew pot. Everybody paid. She was going to have to figure out a solution.

Hurrying to the other side of the room, she opened up the chest and placed the little dog inside. "You sit here and be good," she whispered, patting him on the head.

He lay down, cocking his head as his tail wagged a little slower. But he didn't even whimper as she shut the lid.

A loud hiss followed as the blood fae moved to the nearest open window and glared in at her. Good grief, his shoulders filled the frame. "You will return to me what is mine," he growled.

"He doesn't want to go with you." She removed a cast iron skillet from the wall and tucked it behind her back as she met his gaze. "Go away now."

He folded his arms. "Do you think I'm afraid of you and your pan, human woman? Come out here and face me in the free air if you're so confident in your skills."

"Pass." She strode up to the window and narrowed her eyes at him. "I know better than to go outside on a night like this unless I have to. There are monsters out there."

Usually just dragons and night gryphons. But apparently a blood fae as well.

"Yet you let that thing inside." He glowered at her.

"You mean the puppy?"

"It's not a puppy," he snapped, then covered his face. "It's magic—why am I even trying to explain this to you? It isn't any of your concern."

"I don't know. Seems like a waste of time to me. Besides, the puppy is mine now. You clearly don't have good intentions toward him, so I'm keeping him."

"You can't keep it. It isn't a dog! I need it back to complete my work." He scowled at her window frame, tilting his head. His hair—the palest lavender she had ever seen—slid over his shoulder. "This wood hasn't been consecrated."

Damn that Povro and his careless ways! He'd sworn it was all taken care of.

"Don't you touch this house."

"You touched my apparition. It's only fair." He dug his fingers into the window frame. The wood strained and cracked as the board pulled up.

"Hey! Stop that. Stop that right now!"

"It's hard to stay safe from magic in your house if the house is gone, isn't it, human? Maybe if you hadn't used pine—"

She sprang forward and clubbed him in the side of the head with the cast iron skillet. "Don't tear up my house, you monster!"

With a startled groan, he collapsed against the wooden wall and slid to the ground.

Ha! She knew that iron was their weakness.

But this wasn't going to last for long. If there was a breach in the wood, he could break it apart and get in, and then where would she be? She was going to have to deal with him now while he was down and then figure out a solution.

AN UNUSUAL TRADE

Skillet still in hand, she seized rope from the closet and raced outside.

The lavender-haired fae lay crumpled on the ground, face in the dirt, motionless.

She seized his hands, put them behind his back, and tied them up individually and then together before hogtying him. Good enough for now.

He groaned into the dirt, then swore as she finished. "What is this?"

"You are not welcome in this place," she said, grateful that she was done with the knots. He had woken up faster than she expected.

"So I gathered." He huffed, then started to rock back. "When I get out of this—"

"When you get out of this, you're going to go straight home. I have no intention of harming you. I just don't want you here, so you are going to go away."

She seized his shiny black leather boots. The cuffs and about four inches of his dark-blue trousers were still wet from the creek. Gritting her teeth, she dragged him toward the edge of her wards.

There was a lot to sort out. She'd gotten herself into a fair bit of trouble already, but she'd find a way out and keep the dog.

"Not until I get what I came for," he snarled. He struggled against the ropes, his muscles bunching and tightening. "Believe it or not, I am here for your good."

"I don't believe it."

How had he gotten past the wards? Were they broken? Maybe she needed to ask that kind air elemental to come help her. She'd make a big batch of chicken leek soup with some extra fluffy rolls—or maybe some soda bread—to give in thanks.

"That thing isn't anything real. It's just a magic form. But if you don't let me manage it, it will become real. And then what will you do?"

"Give it treats and a warm bed. It's a puppy."

If she could get him past the creek—well, that actually didn't help.

She halted, still gripping his boots. She had to get him out beyond the wards over her own land. But if she did that, that made her vulnerable to whatever else stalked in the night. Here she was only vulnerable to what flew. But out there…

There was no sense in going any farther until she knew what she was dealing with.

"Were you able to get through here because there was a breach in the wards?"

"No." He scoffed. "I got here because I cut my own path."

"Then why couldn't you come into the house?"

"Houses are different," he muttered.

She scurried in front of him and crouched. "All right. We got off on the wrong foot, I'll grant you that. I do not have anything against you and other blood fae or any fae of any type. I don't want any trouble. I just need to stay safe and keep my home safe. You understand that, right?"

"And I have nothing against humans. Even if one did just club me in the head with a pan. I am not going to hurt anyone. And I don't want to either. But you have to let me take that thing back. I need to take it back and reabsorb the magic."

"That sounds like it would hurt the puppy."

He dropped his forehead against the ground. "It isn't a puppy. It is nothing but dust and dreams and phantoms."

"No. I love him already. He's going to stay with me."

He swore, his face still turned down, his voice muffled by the grass.

"Listen." She remained crouched near him. From this vantage point, he didn't seem nearly so frightening, and if her gut instinct was right, there was a little more to this. Maybe he could be reasoned with. "I'll take good care of him. I'm not going to hurt you. I don't know why you need him, but I'm not going to let anything happen to him. I don't know what to do with you now, though. I don't want to leave you out here all night."

"Well, that won't happen anyway. I'll be out of these ropes soon enough."

"I don't want to drag you off into the wilds either." She gestured toward the edge of her land. The boundary marker was so pale it almost glowed in the moonlight. "I live here at the edge. I sell stew and soup to travelers, no matter who they are. And I don't usually venture past that line. But I know what lies beyond that border. I know it would happily devour you, but I don't wish that on you, even if you would hurt a helpless dog."

"You don't want to drag me across the boundary line because you're afraid for me?" He said this slowly as if mulling it over. A low laugh followed. "Oh, this is ridiculous."

"You're saying that there aren't creatures beyond that would happily devour you?"

"No. They would. If they could. But they won't."

"Yes, because I'm not going to give them the chance. No one deserves to be eaten alive. I don't even cook crabs alive."

"Very noble of you." He tilted his head to glare up at her. His eyes were a deep purple that sparkled silver with flecks of jet and indigo, the moonlight making them seem almost enchanting. "Listen. These ropes won't hold me long. And we both know I can dismantle your house. Why don't we start fresh?"

"Does that mean you'll let me keep the dog?"

"No."

"Then pass."

"What other option do you have?"

"I could hit you with the skillet until you're unconscious?"

"Fair enough. I'll pass on that."

She hesitated. How much longer would the ropes hold him? He didn't seem to be working his wrists or his ankles, but that didn't mean that he wasn't doing anything. His long slender fingers flexed as if he was trying to start some sort of spell or incantation.

Polph. She shouldn't even be out here talking to him beneath a waxing moon. The fuller the moon, the stronger the blood fae, and daylight wouldn't drive him away, even if it might weaken him. All other dangers aside, this wasn't good.

She had to stop him before he managed to create some sort of spell or magic a weapon into existence. But what could she do?

She pressed her lips in a tight line. "I'm sorry!"

"Well, you aren't forgiven—"

She sat on his back and grabbed his hands.

"What are you doing?" he demanded.

"I'm very sorry about this." She threaded her fingers through his. "But I can't have you blood magicking me or anything."

"When I get out of this, do you have any idea what I'm going to do to you?"

"Hopefully, nothing."

He swore again, but he didn't say no. That was probably what he meant, though.

Her stomach fluttered. This was so bad, and it kept getting worse. No one was going to be out this way until morning, and she had just done about half a dozen things that no human should do at any point but especially not at night. The one good thing was that his powers were fairly low right now.

He cleared his throat. "All right. I give up. What's your plan?"

"We're just going to sit here until my friends arrive. Then maybe you'll be reasonable."

"So you aren't going to drag me into the wilds."

"Well, I've been thinking—"

"Seems like a rare thing for you."

She shot him a glare, but she couldn't deny that forethought had not been particularly present in this whole endeavor. "I won't leave you to be eaten or mauled or whatever. So that means you couldn't stay tied up. I am clearly not safe in my house. At least not for tonight. But I don't really have anywhere I could run. Even if I did and even with the head start, I'm not really sure I could outrun you. You have long legs. I think you're probably a fast runner."

"I do not disagree with anything you have said so far."

"Also, sometimes when things spin out of control, I need to sit and just think and figure out a better solution than what I was originally headed toward."

"Fair. I have a solution."

"Oh?"

"Get off me. Untie me. Give me the apparition, and I will leave without doing any harm to you."

"Are you going to kill the dog?"

"It's not a dog!"

"Fine. Are you going to kill it?"

"It isn't alive."

"But it's scared, and killing it wouldn't serve any purpose. You can't do that."

"So your plan is to just sit on me and hold my hands until your friends arrive or something dreadful happens. You realize that you are out in the open at night? Wards won't stop dragons or night eagles. Or gryphons, for that matter. This isn't smart."

"True." She peered up into the sky. "But I don't see or hear anything. Besides, you were here. And you didn't come with protection, so that probably means you knew there wasn't a big risk."

"I didn't plan to be stranded in the open with a human on my back either."

"But you are clearly a somewhat intelligent fae, so you would not have risked it without checking, right?"

More dark mutterings followed.

"Now, as long as we're sitting here, why don't you explain to me just why you can't leave the dog with me?"

"I'd happily leave a dog with you, but that is *not* a dog."

"Fine. The apparition that looks like a dog, feels like a dog, sounds like a dog, and walks like a dog. And that you're going to kill."

"I'm not—I need to get the energy back, all right? I don't have enough. It's very important. I have nothing against the thing. Why do you even care? Why do you want it?"

She kept her fingers threaded through his as she shrugged. "It's scared, and it wants a home. And I have a home."

For now. The pit in her stomach deepened. Nan or Loto weren't likely to kick her out any time soon, but this really was only temporary. If one or more of their granddaughters ever came back from the city, they would take over the soup cottage, and then where would she be? It wasn't as if she had come up with a particularly good plan for her life.

"That's enough, isn't it? Can't you see it's frightened?" she asked.

"I never meant for it to get frightened. That was never supposed to happen. The problem is that the longer the apparition is out, the more it starts to become, —well—real. It probably is in distress now."

"What happens if you don't take it back at all?"

"It will become a real dog. And it will be influenced by the personality and the life force of those nearest it. Though I doubt it'll have much to do with what it was supposed to be originally."

"What was it supposed to be originally?"

He stared down at the ground, his shoulders rigid.

She tilted her head. "What were you trying to create that you made such a cute dog by accident?"

"A winged garm." He huffed.

"A garm?"

She glanced back over her shoulder at the house. The door was still open, and the little dog with the crooked wings was now at the threshold. Apparently, he'd figured out how to escape the chest.

"If that's what you were trying to create, then you really did fail. I don't think he looks remotely wolf-like."

The blood fae shook his head, his silky hair shining in the moonlight. "Oh, you noticed that, did you?"

"Just because he isn't ferocious doesn't mean he doesn't deserve to live."

"Now, listen to me. If it turned out that he really was a real dog, I wouldn't harm him. But I need a garm. This isn't magic that I want to practice, but it is essential. There's no point for an apparition who just looks cute. Even if it does turn into a real dog...eventually."

She leaned back, her hands tightening around his. That was an odd thing to say. He sounded almost sad when he said it.

"What should I call you?" she asked.

"Oh, are we at the stage for exchanging names?"

"You can call me Erryn."

"Ryul."

She smiled. "I figured it'd be something like Prince Blood Bath or Lord Clotting Veins."

"Well, it doesn't feel like we're on particularly formal terms right now. Also, no one has a name that stupid."

"Are you in pain right now, Ryul?"

He scoffed. "Would you let me go if I was?"

"I'd try to make it better. I know this is unpleasant and awkward."

"I'm wonderful."

"All right." She nodded. "Well, Ryul, I think that the point of that dog is that he is him. He doesn't have to be a wolf or terrifying or any such thing. He just exists, and I love him."

"You do not. You cannot actually love that thing."

"Actually, I can. And you don't know me, so don't make assumptions. I think we can agree that your apparition has gone on too long. Even if it wasn't supposed to have feelings or become real, it is now, so you can't kill it. But you need your magic replenished?"

"Are you suggesting we make a deal?"

Her stomach tightened. She hated that word, and she'd vowed she would never under any circumstances make a deal with a fae. Not after what happened the last time.

She swallowed hard. "A—a trade. What about a trade?"

He tried to glance back at her. "Is something wrong? You don't sound right."

"I'm fine." She cleared her throat. "What about a trade?"

"What's the difference between a trade and a bargain?"

"Trades involve specific terms that are precise. Bargains are more open-ended."

"Really?"

"Yes." She drew in a deep breath. "What does it take to replenish your magic?"

"I don't—I don't actually know. At least not beyond taking back the apparition and putting it back through the process."

"Well, I have heard that fae can regenerate magic over time. And that the right foods could make it happen faster."

"I've heard the same, but I don't actually know what they are. Do you?"

"I can find out or at least try, but I'd be willing to make you soup every night for at least three months until we get you something that works if you let me keep the dog."

"You want to trade soup for a dog—apparition?"

"I make excellent soup."

He remained silent a moment longer. "This is ridiculous. You know that."

"A little."

"And if I wanted to hurt you, I'd just break free and sit on you."

"I imagine if you could get free, you'd have done so already." She glanced up at the sky, scanning for any dark shapes or reasons to be concerned. "But I accept that you don't want to hurt me."

Even if she wasn't entirely certain she believed him. He didn't sound nearly so angry as she would have expected.

"Are you willing to make the trade? I make you soup, and you let me keep the dog?"

"If I agree to this, it doesn't even matter if you follow through," he said. "I can't get the magic back from the apparition after the form has fully set. But..."

He studied her, his head cocked at an awkward angle. His hair had slid over half his face, hiding one eye and leaving his sharply pointed ear exposed.

What was he trying to determine?

She met his gaze. It wasn't a good trade. Not really, but she couldn't let something happen to that dog.

Sighing, he shook his head. "Fine. I accept the terms of your barg—"

"Trade," she corrected.

"Trade." He frowned.

"You swear that you will not harm me or the dog?"

"I swear."

"Do you want me to swear something about the soup?"

"No. I'd like you to untie me."

This seemed a little odd. Then again, the more she thought about it, the stranger the situation was.

She frowned then, realizing something else. "Why don't you have fangs?"

He scowled. "That's a rude thing to ask."

"I'm sorry. I just—I just noticed. How do I know you won't attack me after I untie you?"

He'd gone down so easily too. It really hadn't been that hard to best him. Maybe he was sick somehow? He certainly didn't look it, though.

"Because I am bound by my word?" He raised an eyebrow, his expression pure confusion. "Is there some other way you would like me to swear it? I swear I won't harm you in any way. All right? Satisfied? Now untie me. This is unseemly."

Her gut tightened. Fae were dangerous. Tricky. Full of deceit. A lot like humans but a lot more clever. Still, he hadn't really been that bad in their conversation. He hadn't threatened her personally once. He'd made a vow.

And—she tilted her head back to take in the night sky.

The cloud cover was intensifying as the moon slid through the darkness. Best get it over with. She undid the knots and then jumped back, ready to dash into the house.

Pushing himself up, he stood.

He really was tall.

He rubbed his wrists as he glowered at her. "I'll return for my soup. Make sure it lives up to your claims."

"You'll be delighted," she said, a little more confidently than she felt. She slipped back closer to the door. "I make wonderful soup."

He grunted. "You realize if I were—" He stopped, then shook his head. "I'm sure it will be adequate, though I'm not convinced it will restore my magic. You're getting off far better with this deal, you know, but don't think I'm doing you a favor. And don't you dare fall in love with me."

"You think I would fall in love with you?" She blinked, then laughed. "I just offered to make you soup to restore your magic so I can keep the dog. I'm not going to marry you. Why would you even say that?"

"Because—" He stopped, then rubbed his eyes. "It's been a long night. I just don't want more complications, all right? I'm not here that long. As soon as my magic is restored, I have to leave. That's why I needed the dog—I mean, apparition—so your soup—" He sighed, then tossed a glare at the dog. "Probably wouldn't have worked anyway." He brushed the dirt from his jacket and then straightened it with a snap. "Until we meet again, human."

He strode away like a cat who had fallen and was

trying to pretend that was precisely what it had intended to do all along.

She ducked back into the house, scooped up the dog, and then watched Ryul through the window.

There had been a lot of risks this night. She hadn't been the brightest.

But she had a dog now.

The little pup wiggled and squirmed, licking at her face.

Not really a dog? She frowned, almost laughing. She really wasn't fond of magic, and she certainly didn't know all the ins and outs. But how could this little creature just be something made of magic? How could he be anything but real?

As if he heard her, the little dog nuzzled her cheek. His tail continued to wag, striking her arm as she held him close. He smelled like river water and chestnuts.

"Yes, you're a real dog, for sure," she cooed. "You're a real dog, and like any real dog, you need a good name."

Cute or funny names for pets had always amused her as a girl. And given his appearance, how could she give him anything but a silly name?

"What should it be? Buttons? Noodle? Biscuit? Pickles? Potato?"

He gave a low growl-yip.

What a strange day.

She ladled up some broth from the pot that simmered over the low fire and cooled it with a touch of water before giving it to him. As he lapped it up, she checked the door and made sure everything was ready for her to rest.

What a night.

She washed her face and then patted it dry with a towel. By that point, the little dog had returned to her side. If he wasn't a dog yet, he certainly acted like it. When she stretched out on the bed, he hopped up beside her, placed his head on her chest, and closed his eyes.

Strange as it was, the day had turned out all right. And that bizarre blood fae—well, he hadn't done nearly as much to her as he might have. The trade didn't require it, but she would find some way to thank him. And now—thank all that was good—she had a dog all her own.

"Buttons, I think," she whispered.

He licked her nose.

"Do you like that name?"

She hugged the little beast closer and drifted into dreamless slumber. Even with the heat and the humidity, she didn't mind him being close. Life had gotten better. Even if some parts remained uncertain.

HEALING SOUP

A full roster of chores required Erryn's attention as soon as she woke, and Buttons had his own needs, including time out in the grass, a little run, exploration, play, and, of course, food and water.

He scurried about, wagging his tail so hard that his whole body moved. He barely held still long enough to eat the shredded chicken and broth she gave him for his breakfast. For not being a real dog to start off, he certainly acted like it right now. He even sat, scratched behind his ear with his little hind leg, and nearly toppled himself into a blackberry bush like a real dog.

As much as she would have liked to spend all morning playing with him and watching him explore his new home, she had to get to work on the soup.

The broth in the large pots had simmered all night, both in the cauldron over the fireplace, where she prepared her special broth, and the pots on the stove. The riverstone fireplace took up a good portion of one wall. The woodstove directly beside it could hold up to six pots of soup at a time.

Come midday, her customers would begin arriving. Some would bring their own large containers with heavy lids to transport the soup for their businesses or homes or travels. A few regulars rotated through containers here at her little shop. She always stocked a few extras for the travelers who stopped through who just needed some food before starting off into the wilds.

It was a simple job. Rarely did anyone have any special or unusual requests for her. The soups were usually variations of vegetable soup, bird and barley, and seasonal soups. Those were Nan's standard recipes. Erryn had made these so many times at this point she could do it in her sleep, but that meant she had more time to pore over the cookbooks Nan had left her.

Those dusty old books sat on the shelf on the eastern wall. They had autumnal-colored bindings of faded leather with thin pages. When she had first gotten here, she had taken each one down and looked through, delighted to see all the distinct recipes and notations for their various purposes. Then, all too swiftly, she had discovered that she was only expected to make those basic recipes, the ones on the plain cards in the top drawer on the far-left counter.

Not that she had complained. Nan and Loto had given her a place to stay as well as a livelihood for the time being. It was generous.

But now, she had a purpose for going through those beautiful books once more.

By late morning, all the ingredients for the main soups had been chopped, and the soups themselves simmered on the stovetop. The massive pots steamed and bubbled, making her grateful for the open windows and the constant steady breeze.

She prepped the containers for pickup and ladled up the standing orders. Next would come the couriers. She put Buttons back in the bedroom and closed the door so he wouldn't be underfoot or raise uncomfortable questions about where she had gotten him. Then, she propped the main door open with a coarse green stone, and one by one, the couriers and customers came by, trickling in at a comfortable pace. Most were regulars who stopped in at least once a week, so she knew them decently well. If any of them were knowledgeable about such things, she asked for help tracking down ingredients or information about what could be done to improve or restore fae magic. When they asked why she needed such knowledge, she said it was just for a possible business opportunity in the future and her own curiosity.

Povro was one of the customers, though not one she asked for help in restoring fae magic. He was a pleasant-faced man with ruddy cheeks and wide-set blue eyes. Despite his occasional error—such as failing to properly consecrate the windowsills and his tendency to cut corners—he was impossible to dislike. Mostly because no one had died because of his errors. At least, not yet.

Though he was almost always in a good mood, his new friend, a red-cloaked man with a pheasant-feathered hat appeared to put him in even better humor than usual.

"Erryn, come over here. Come meet Traelan." Povro indicated the newcomer.

Traelan had loosely curled red-brown hair and bright-green eyes that sparkled. There was something rather unnatural about him. Fae or elf or shifter, perhaps. She'd never been particularly good at identifying the different races when their defining traits weren't on display. Still, his features were strong and chiseled, his skin tanned from hours spent in the sun. He moved with grace and confidence as if he owned every step he took, and now, he surveyed the cottage with an air of someone appraising the value.

"Traelan." Erryn dipped her head forward in greeting, offering a mild smile in response. "Povro, your chicken soup is there, but I need to see you privately at some point. It's important."

"Anything you need to say to me, feel free to say in front of my friend." Povro grinned as he picked up the large wooden container filled with steaming soup. "He's a locksmith, a runic cartographer, and an artifact hunter, among other things."

"None of which matters at the moment. For now, I'm just a traveler." Traelan gave her a far more charming smile than she warranted, his eyes twinkling. "But if the young woman needs to speak with you, I will not intrude. I'll examine the runes on the boundary markers."

"I'll see you shortly then." Povro waited until he disappeared out the door and beyond the hickory tree to return his focus to her. "You should be nicer to him. He's a real charmer."

"I'm sure he is." She folded her arms. Povro thought everyone was charming and good unless circumstances showed otherwise. "But I'd rather the magical protections and wards around my home not be a subject of discussion."

"It isn't his type of magic anyway."

"Doesn't matter. But speaking of magic, I need you to treat the windowsills. They aren't properly warded, and that needs to be fixed immediately."

"Aren't they?" He scratched the top of his head, tousling his sandy-brown hair. "Huh. Could have sworn I did."

"I can assure you that you didn't, so please make sure that is dealt with. Before tonight."

She needed to be ready for Ryul to return before sunrise to get his soup. Was that how it was going to be? She hadn't worked out the details with him about how he would get the soup or a delivery method, and she wasn't certain where he was staying actually.

"Before tonight? Why? There aren't any blood fae or lich or anything else like that out this way."

She frowned. Odd that he didn't know about Ryul. Povro tended to know about most things. Maybe Ryul was keeping things quiet. It didn't feel right to mention his presence, and it really didn't matter. The windowsills needed to be treated regardless.

"I don't like being vulnerable, and if something goes wrong, it isn't as if they would leave calling cards before attacking. Will you take care of it, please?"

"Sure. No need to concern yourself with it at all. I'll get Traelan to his lodgings, and then I'll pick up the herbs and dye. So before dinner." He winked at her as he stepped back. "No need to be concerned at all."

People like Povro never seemed to worry too much, but that wasn't her.

She lifted her hand to wave farewell as he left as she took one more glance at the red-cloaked stranger. That was someone to keep an eye on.

He, too, glanced around, though, and when he caught her looking at him, he tapped his fingers to his hat and grinned. She simply waved in response. He reminded her of the kind of man she'd fallen for in her travels. Easy with the words and quick with the smiles but hard on the feelings.

Her body tensed, and she closed her eyes, trying to push those memories away. She'd been an idiot far too many times in her past.

A rap at the door broke her contemplation. Lanna Whiteclaw fluttered her fire-scarred fingers. "Vegetable soup ready?"

"For you, always." She brought her smile back and stepped behind the counter to pick up a smaller wooden container filled with vegetable soup.

Lanna gave her the old container along with the coin.

By mid-afternoon, everyone had come through. She refilled the water jugs and the pots for the next day's broth as well as that night's soup. Too dangerous to do that after dark, even without a blood fae coming. Then she slipped in to take care of Buttons, scratching under his chin and refilling his water bowl. No one needed to know about him. Eventually, she'd have to figure out a way to explain this little fella. Maybe just that she had found him. She was right beside the Barrens Wild, after all.

Yes. That would work, wouldn't it?

Though maybe not with Traelan. If her gut was right, he was someone who would be hard to fool.

Just to be safe, she waited until after Povro came and treated the windowsills. Then she took Buttons out for a run and some play. After he'd wearied himself, she returned indoors, pulled down the dusty old books, and sat down with the little dog.

Buttons curled up in her lap as she read, behaving far more like a cat than a dog. She didn't mind, even with the humidity and warmth in the house. He rolled onto his back so she could scratch his patchy black tummy and rub the scales along his sides.

Despite the fact that an annoyed blood fae was going to come visit her soon, she didn't feel so bad. Life was much better with a dog. This had been a good decision. A good trade. And she would find the answer to restoring his magic. Even if he didn't expect all that much of her.

She pored over the cookbooks. There were so many theories of magic and replenishing, but none were more than passing references and general concepts aside from an overall belief that, for those who generated magic, it was simple enough to replenish with the right ingredients. Not that any of them said what specific ingredients aside from "all magic types and subtypes respond best to particular sets" and "rosemary and garlic are standard in most."

Well, those she did have. Who knew what exactly they did for magic though? Probably nothing bad, considering all the soup she had made for all kinds of fae over the years.

Standing, she crossed over to the slab counter and laid out all the books. The remnants of the soup and broth still simmered. She needed to get started on preparations for tomorrow and prepare a new pot of soup for Ryul.

Resting her hands on the top of her head, she sighed. Maybe just starting with something basic would be wise. Garlic chicken and rosemary with root vegetables. If he arrived an hour or so before dawn, it would be practically perfect, and she already had a chicken prepared in the icebox.

Polph, this had to work. Where had the time even gone? The sun had already set.

Buttons leaned against her leg, gazing up at her adoringly.

"Don't worry," she said. "I'll figure it out."

A shadow passed over the windowsill. Ryul stood as close as he could, his broad shoulders almost filing the frame. "Have you made it yet?" he demanded.

She raised an eyebrow as she put out the onions, garlic, celery, sweet potatoes, yellow potatoes, pink turnips, old carrots, and thin parsnips. With each subsequent item, she stacked them higher. What was he doing here? Not that she had said he shouldn't come at this time. See, this was why it was dangerous to deal with fae. She hadn't thought to specify the time.

"What does it look like, blood fae?"

"Good." He folded his arms, his gaze tight on her. "Because I'm not eating anything I don't watch you prepare."

"You're going to watch me prepare soup?" She raised her eyebrow even higher. "Do you think I'm going to poison you?"

"I wouldn't put it past you," he said coolly.

She found a mischievous smile pulling at her mouth as she adjusted her broad white apron. Faint soup stains across the front indicated so many pots of soup over the past few years. Most had faded from memory, but she was probably going to remember this one even without an interesting stain.

"First, if I wanted to poison you, I would probably have already done it. Second, I would never put poison in one of my soups. Cupcakes, maybe. My business doesn't revolve around them. Third, if I did decide to poison the soup, you wouldn't know until it was too late. There are far too many ingredients in here for you to know all of them, and you won't be able to follow my every move."

"You do your part, and I'll do mine."

"So does that mean you don't want me to poison you? I would appreciate clarity about what this soup is supposed to do."

His brow tweaked as if he was either offended or surprised. "No. Don't poison me. Just fix my magic. If you can."

"Well, I'll do my best. You just can't come in."

"Fine. I don't want to come into your shabby little cottage anyway." He folded his arms as he glared in at her through the window.

She pulled out her cutting board and then removed one of her favorite knives. Gesturing toward him with the blade, she shrugged. "Besides, I wouldn't even begin to know how to poison a blood fae."

"But you know how to replenish my magic with soup?"

"I said I would try to figure out a way, and I made no guarantees. Just best effort." She started slicing up the onions. "And you agreed to it."

"You sounded more confident last night." He then shook his head as he folded his arms. "Not that it matters," he muttered, casting another look at the dog.

"His name is Buttons."

He rolled his eyes. "Why? Why would you name him that?"

"You think he should have another name? What would you name him?" She raised an eyebrow at him.

He grumbled, the words indistinct.

Buttons cocked his head, then yipped at him.

"Yes, I know you are a real dog now. Stupid curse." He looked up at her then. "You do know that you'll have to feed him. Just because he is magic doesn't mean he doesn't need real food."

"Really?" She smirked. "Does he need water?"

"Yes! Have you not given him water in this heat?" He stopped short, then lifted his chin. With a sharp clearing of his throat, he continued, his tone far calmer. "You're teasing me, aren't you?"

She twitched her shoulder at him as she continued chopping. This was one of her favorite parts of making soup. The neat and even slices. She'd gotten fairly quick at this over the years.

"Maybe. But yes, set your mind at ease. I have fed him and given him water."

"And let him play?" He sounded a little more tentative.

"You know, for someone who was going to reabsorb the apparition in some way, you seem very concerned."

"If he's going to be a real dog, he should be treated like a real dog. Well, treated like a real dog who is treated well."

"Even if he's not a garm?"

He scoffed, then nodded. His arms remained folded tight over his chest. "Even if he's useless." He started to lean forward on the windowsill, then pulled back. "Oh. You changed it."

He'd noticed that windowsill fast.

Was he hurt? He sounded a little hurt.

She almost apologized but caught herself. "It's going to take a while for me to finish this soup. Do you want me to pass you a chair through the window so you can sit on something?"

"It's fine." He rubbed his arm as he stared down at the floor. "It was wise anyway."

It was. But now it felt awkward. She restrained a sigh. This was going to be a long night if he insisted on staying there the whole time.

But no matter what she offered, he refused to leave, and she couldn't exactly blame him.

She explained each ingredient as she added it in. As it simmered, she started the cleanup. Buttons trotted around with her, cocking his head and sniffing everything.

"Is it a secret that you're here?" she asked.

"Me?" Ryul tilted his head. For a moment, his expression reminded her of the little dog. Almost guilty. "Why do you want to know that?"

"Well, I don't know too many blood fae, but usually when they are around, people know. They aren't subtle. And someone who ordinarily would know didn't know about you."

"Did you tell that someone about me?" An odd tenseness filled his voice.

"No." She still wasn't entirely certain why she had kept that quiet.

He breathed a little easier. "Thank you."

"Are you wanted for something?"

He'd said he was from a noble family, and his clothing certainly confirmed that.

"Not so much wanted as unwanted," he responded. His fingers tapped against his arm as he kept them crossed at his chest. "But I won't be here long. Just until I can sort out my magic and get my strength back. Then I'll be gone." He hesitated, his gaze hardening. "It would be best if you didn't tell anyone I was here or who my family is."

"I didn't even know your name before you told me. I certainly don't know your family's, but I can understand wanting privacy." She crossed over in front of the window though she remained out of arm's reach. "Who is your family?"

He opened his mouth to speak, then frowned and shook his head. "It doesn't matter now."

A sadness clung to those words. She bit the inside of her lip. Some part of her recognized the longing, and before she could stop herself, she blurted out, "Are you looking for them?"

He started, then hesitated. Slowly, he nodded. "Yes. I have been for a while now."

"What was Buttons supposed to do?"

"What any garm is supposed to do. Track and protect."

Buttons yipped, sitting up on his hind legs. His wings twitched.

Ryul rolled his eyes. "Not that it matters."

Erryn picked up Buttons and scratched his tummy. "We'll get your magic back up to its full strength. And I won't tell anyone that you're here. Also, Buttons is perfect just the way he is."

"Well, I won't be here. Not during the daylight hours at least. And at night, well..." He shrugged. "It doesn't matter. Your soup does not smell dreadful, though."

"My soup smells wonderful, and it tastes even better. Though I suppose I should ask, what is your favorite kind?"

Maybe there was a clue there.

He shrugged again, his expression twitching. "Whatever kind is available and hot."

"That opens up a lot of possibilities."

"One would think." The silence grew heavier for a moment before he nodded at her. "What about you?"

"I like trying new combinations. New things. Not that that happens so much here. So if it had to be a staple, it would be venison and vegetable soup."

"And you're here all alone? No family either?"

"No family here. I lost them a long time ago."

"I'm sorry."

She shook her head. Tears misted over her eyes as she forced a smile. "It's fine. It doesn't matter. I don't even remember what happened."

Oh. The lie came so quickly and easily now. He hadn't even asked for details. Why was she talking?

"You don't?" Ryul's expression grew contemplative. "That would be awful."

Sometimes the truth was worse.

She tried to wave the words away, but they kept coming. The distinct blending of fact and fiction that had become her story for the past several years. "Nan found me on one of the staircases in the forest. She's the one who owns this place. She found me and took me back to her home, and she and her husband decided I could run this soup cottage until one of their granddaughters was ready to come back from the city. Simple as that. No dark memories. No tragedies. Nothing like that."

"Still, it would be hard not knowing. Not even remembering their faces."

Her stomach clenched. The tears wanted to return.

She just shook her head though. "Sometimes we just have to make do with what we have."

"It's lonely though," he said. "Not having your family or people you picked as your family."

"That's what friends are for." She set Buttons down. "And dogs, for that matter. Now, are you ready for some soup?"

"Yes."

She lifted the lid and gave it one more stir. Rosemary garlic chicken soup was a simple recipe for starting with. Her grandmother had always insisted it made you healthier and stronger. And her mother had made it at least once a month every autumn and winter.

She ladled a steaming portion into a large brown bowl and then placed it with a spoon on the wooden peel used for putting loaves into the brick oven. Carefully, she slid it over to the window and out beyond the warding.

"Here."

He accepted it, his fingers wrapping around the carved bowl as if he did not even feel the heat. "Thank you."

"You're welcome." She drew the peel back in and set it aside.

Hopefully, this worked and fast. This blood fae was already making her say more than she should, and she didn't know why it was so hard to contain anything around him. Sooner or later, she'd probably tell him everything. And then where would she be?

Ryul's eyes lit up as he took the first bite. Then he masked his expression. "It's decent."

"Decent?" She crossed her arms now, not even trying to hide her smile. "Is that all you have to say? That's great soup."

He took another bite, no longer looking at her. "Well, maybe..." he murmured. He scowled. "Aren't you going to eat any?"

Surprised, she tilted her head. "I—"

"You should."

"To prove it isn't poisoned?"

"No." His brow tweaked again. "I would have mentioned it before I ate some if I really thought that. But you must be hungry too."

Not really, but she hadn't eaten all day. It was easy to forget with everything else that was going on.

She dished up her own bowl and came to stand across from him.

The taste took her back home almost at once, again summoning tears. It wasn't quite the same as her mother's. Nothing ever could be. She cradled the bowl a little closer and then took another bite. It had been far too long since she had made this.

Ryul finished his second bowl and tentatively requested thirds. As she brought it back, he studied her. "Do you need to talk about something?"

"Why?" She placed the bowl on the peel and offered it through the open window once more.

"Just—you seem sad."

"It's just the onions and the garlic. They make my eyes water."

"Oh." He didn't sound convinced. With the spoon in one hand and the bowl situated on his palm, he stared down at the broth. "Well, that's good then."

He then resumed eating, his pace increasing. She had barely finished her first bowl when he requested a fourth. Then a fifth. He must have been hollow because that was the only way she could figure he was able to put so much away.

By the time the moon had started to slide behind the trees, he had finished off the last of the soup in the pot. "I really didn't know what to expect when we made this bargain—"

"Trade," she corrected.

"Trade." He set the bowl back on the windowsill. "Anyway, it was delicious."

"Did it work then?"

He hesitated. The brashness that had emerged momentarily faded from his expression. Then he smiled and shrugged. "Maybe it takes a little longer for the effects to be felt. It was truly delicious though. And it was good to be able to eat with someone again."

"Come back tomorrow night, and I'll fix a different type. We'll figure out how to make your magic strong again."

"I'll see you tomorrow." He nodded, then strode away, his pace stronger.

SMALL FAVORS

Erryn only managed to catch a couple hours of sleep before dawn's light streamed through the window. Buttons nudged up under her arm, eager to get outside. She spent a little longer out in the fresh air and rapidly warming sunshine. Buttons didn't want to run too far, but he enjoyed chasing the stick and following along with her as she went about her business.

It was an ordinary day. She tended to her chores in the morning and prepared the soup. Buttons explored the cottage with even more vigor, chewing on any wooden leg he could find. A little before the couriers and customers were set to come, she put him in her bedroom once more with a big bowl of water and some sticks to chew on.

"Be a good boy and keep quiet like yesterday," she said, scratching behind his ears.

He panted, then laid down again, watching her with wide, dark-red eyes.

Yesterday, he had been so well-behaved. Hopefully today, he would be the same.

She closed the door firmly behind her, grateful that the bedroom was in the back of the little cottage so that those who came to pick up the soup would not see him unless they were creeping around and peeping through the curtains.

The usual cycle started just minutes after she opened the front door, Margo Terr appearing with her green gloves and her purple wooden container and a soft rap on the open door. A small cannister of chicken vegetable soup and a little chitchat later, and off she went. Two more regulars replaced her—Varnol for two large containers of vegetable soup and Coleman for two smaller cannisters of dark bone broth.

Light conversation followed and flowed, usually about the weather and the time of year, casual topics that had no particular depth to them and which she scarcely paid attention to.

A couple strangers passed through as well, ragged and worn from walking. They each ordered a bowl of soup and asked if they could eat it by the creek. Of course, she agreed.

The woman with the tattered blue hat thanked her. "It'll be good to have a moment. It's hard in the wilds. Places like this are a godsend."

"It isn't so bad," said her companion. "Usually the predators are far worse. Barely seen a tenth of the biters or monsters since we got past the south band of the Barrens Wild."

Erryn smiled in response. "Glad to hear it. If you need anything, just let me know."

By late afternoon, most business had concluded. She kept the door open though just in case. It was a little too early, and the heat was getting to her. She'd practically finished off two pitchers of water on her own, and the sweat made her pale-blue dress stick to her body as if it had been plastered on.

Whenever possible, she'd taken little peeks in at Buttons, relieved to find him calm and comfortable, resting with his head on his paws just beneath the bed as if this temperature was the most normal thing in the world. She refilled his water bowl, gave him another kiss on the head, and returned to the kitchen.

What kind of soup should she make for tonight?

The rosemary garlic chicken hadn't worked, but maybe white beans with pork and thyme? She could get the white beans started soaking now. The book stated that thyme helped many cultivate strength and encouraged protection. That might translate to restoration of magical powers, right?

Better than nothing. Besides, she had some extra pork bones from the last delivery.

She made the preparations, using up the last of one pitcher and all but a third of the other to start soaking the beans. A sharp rap on the door startled her almost to dropping it.

"Hello there." Traelan stood in the doorway, wearing the same vibrant cloak and hat as the day before but with different garb beneath. A dark blue doublet with charcoal grey trousers and a silver baldric with a series of runes carved into the metal buckle. "You're still open for business?"

She hugged the carafe close and scowled. "You need soup?"

"What do you have left? I know it's rather late in the day for new orders."

"Same as yesterday except we're all out of vegetable." She rattled off the usual line-up, her heart still racing.

There was something about him that seemed very familiar. As if she should know him. Not that he would be easy to forget. His piercing eyes and the sharp clothing all made him difficult to miss. Was it really just because she'd run into his type before?

"Ah, alas. Vegetable is precisely what I was hoping for. Well, it will teach me to come so late or to not put in an order." He glanced around the cottage's interior, then sniffed the air. "Tell me." His brow wrinkled. "Has a blood fae passed through this way?"

She blinked, feigning innocence as she placed the pitcher back on the counter. "That's a rather specific question. You can—you can smell different types of fae?"

"My sense of smell is exceptional. I smell blood fae magic. One has been here, practicing their magic."

She shrugged. "A lot of people pass through. I don't know how to recognize all the races on sight. And I definitely can't smell them like you apparently can."

"You'd notice a blood fae though, I'm certain. Especially as this is warded against undesired entry. Besides, beyond that, this magic smells raw. Unfinished. Lacking." He frowned, his brow creasing with three thin lines. His gaze traveled around the room. "Do you mind if I search the cottage?"

"I do mind, actually. This is my home, and everything is fine. I don't need you sniffing around." She gave the wooden spoon a solid rap on the side of the pot. "Like Povro said, there are no blood fae here. And even if there were, everything is secured against them and a lot of other things that might cause me or anyone else harm."

"Yes. Povro mentioned you asked him to come and treat the windowsills."

Damn Povro.

She steeled her smile and gave a slight nod. No chance of casually asking whether he knew how one might restore blood fae magic. "So I did."

"Against blood fae."

"Against anything that might cross and which might be repelled with his particular blend. Don't let appearances deceive you. He's a bit of a genius when it comes to that sort of thing."

"How did you come to realize that your home was lacking in this manner?"

She lifted a shoulder. "I know Povro. I figured it out. He's a good man, but he does tend to miss things."

"Yes. But for you to conclude the windowsill specifically—"

"Listen, I'm not trying to be rude. But why do you care?"

"I wouldn't want to see you get hurt. Blood fae can get nasty. They don't even need the blood magic.

Even with their mates, they exact a horrifying toll simply at the confession of love. There are few that compare to them with their puppetry and monstrousness."

"You speak as if you have personal experience with them."

"I do. And I would hate to see someone so lovely fall prey to them."

She smirked. No one called her lovely these days unless they wanted something.

"Leave off the flattery. What do you want from me exactly?"

"Any information about any blood fae you might find. Their magic. Their icons. Their possessions. Anything."

"And what are you going to do with it?"

He smiled, the expression so easy on his face and yet not quite reaching his eyes. "Setting certain wrongs right, my dear. Nothing more. Many have been lost or harmed by blood fae over the years. They can control your blood as it pumps in your veins."

Not if you hit them in the head with a cast iron skillet they couldn't.

"They are swift. Masters of manipulation. The venom in their fangs can sedate or kill, depending on the type and decision. And they are so charming you might not even care until it was too late."

"I've heard the stories." She set the spoon aside as she folded her arms over her broth-stained apron. "But the cottage is protected. Povro told you that himself. And I don't trust strangers quickly. So while it has been such a treat chatting with you, it's time for me to close up and take some time to myself."

"Of course. Thank you for your time." His smile didn't even waver a little bit as he tipped his hat to her and strode away. He passed over the threshold, then turned. "If you should change your mind or find that you do realize there is a blood fae nearby, please inform me at once."

"If there's anything you need to know, I'll certainly pass it on." She closed the door behind him, then stood in front of it, her hands on her waist.

Her stomach refused to calm.

Buttons would have to remain hidden until that stranger left. No chance of pretending she found him in the wilds, was there? Even though she had perfected her own fabricated background and the fact that she couldn't remember anything about who she was before Nan found her, the lies had worked largely because no one cared to press too hard on the facts. The stairways to nowhere in the forest were known for their damaging effects and memory erasure as well as worse side effects. They appeared at random. No one could control them or understand them.

At least, no one she knew.

So a girl in rags with a dead-shock stare and an unwillingness to speak found on the staircase didn't seem that unusual. No one questioned why she panicked when people started yelling or at over-loud voices. It helped that it wasn't yelling the way Ryul did it. Even when he had been upset, it hadn't been full of rage and loathing. Nor had it filled her ears like—

She ducked her head. No. She had to stop this train of thought. It wasn't helping. What mattered for now was what she told Traelan. What would he believe?

Traelan—well—he was obviously suspicious about something. If he could smell blood fae magic, how likely was it that he wouldn't recognize Buttons as a blood fae apparition turned into a dog?

She rubbed her hand over her mouth.

This wasn't good. What would he do if he found out the truth? Would he turn on her? Would he take Buttons away? Maybe it would be better to just admit that Ryul had been here but had left.

No. She shook her head.

Ryul might be a blood fae, but it wouldn't be right to turn him in or speak about him. Blood fae could be dangerous, but that was true of most races who came this way. Peace thrived in these parts largely because people kept to themselves. They didn't interfere with other people's business. Travelers like Traelan could be just as dangerous, if not more so.

Scoffing, she drew her hands up over her eyes and then released a long breath.

Under no circumstances would she trust either of them. She wasn't an idiot, no matter what some might think. There wasn't anything about Ryul that kept her from trusting. She wouldn't trust most people here, on the road, or in the wilds if she could help it.

Besides, she'd made a trade with Ryul. She might lie about a lot of things, but she kept her promises.

Polph. She needed this to not be so difficult. Was there a way to counter the smell of blood fae magic?

Peeking out the window, she satisfied herself that Traelan was gone. Then she let Buttons out, ran back to the books, and began searching for scents that could cover magic. How would she even know if it was working? She couldn't smell blood fae magic at all. Lighting a candle, she set it next to the books and pulled up a stool.

Buttons pawed at her leg, asking to be held. Scooping him up, she kept reading.

"There has to be something," she whispered. "I'm not going to let anyone find you and take you away, baby boy. All right? No one."

He licked her chin.

She kissed the top of his head and resumed scanning the indexes. Nothing. Useless. Not helpful. *Nothing*.

Groaning, she hugged Buttons closer. "There's got to be a way."

"A way for what?"

Jumping, she gasped. Then she glared as she closed the book with a steady hand.

"Nothing. I just didn't hear you come up."

Ryul was at the window once more. His stare didn't seem quite so sullen.

Picking up the beans, she drained out the water they'd been soaking in and then poured the beans into the pot of broth and bones.

"I'm just getting ready to make tonight's soup. White beans with pork and thyme, and—" She halted, realizing she had in fact forgotten to get the water. And she'd just poured out the water the beans had soaked in.

He tilted his head. "What's wrong?"

She set her hands on her waist, her fingers curving around the coarse ties of her apron. "It's nothing."

"Doesn't look like it's nothing." He glanced back over his shoulder as if that might offer some insight, then looked back at her. "You're upset?"

"No."

There was a solution. There had to be. She had a quart of milk in the icebox and whatever was in the pitcher, but even combined, that wouldn't make more than half a pot. And opening up the well at night when you were human...

She closed her eyes, suppressing a shudder. And that was assuming Ryul didn't pull anything. How likely was that, anyway? He was a blood fae who had been jumped and essentially tricked into giving up a magical manifestation of his powers that had become a dog. How likely was he to—

Buttons barked.

Something liquid sloshed near the window.

She opened her eyes.

Ryul stood at the open window with a large bucket of water in hand. "Is this what you need?"

She hesitated, fingers tightening as she studied him. Was there some sort of trick here? Why had he done that?

He gave the bucket a small shake. Some more water spilled out. "If you don't want it, let me know."

She stepped closer. "And what do you want in return?"

"Nothing." He scowled. "It isn't like you can make soup without liquid. Especially not beans."

"No." She continued to study him, noting the almost hesitancy in his expression. But there was also an openness. Those amethyst eyes seemed very young and very sincere right now. "You didn't do anything to it?"

He rolled his eyes, then sighed and laughed. "Just watch." He poured the water out and returned to the well.

Blinking, she hurried to the window. What was he doing?

As he reached the well, he set the bucket down. Then he lifted the wooden lid. A long purple tentacle shot up, moving as if to coil around him. He didn't even flinch. Just lifted his hand and flexed two fingers. A bright burst of red and purple energy flared around the tentacle. It slid down out of sight. He then lowered the gathering bucket into the well.

That was actually—that was kind. And he hadn't killed the squid. He'd just sent it back down into the well where it belonged.

He emptied the now-full bucket into his own and returned to her. "See?" He placed it on the windowsill. "No tricks."

"Thank you." She edged closer, her gaze fixed on him. Was he pleased? Was it possible there was some trick that she hadn't thought of?

His brow tweaked. "Are you going to take it?"

"No poison or anything like that?"

"You watched me. Aren't your eyes fast enough?" He smiled a little.

"Why would you get that for me?"

He shrugged but dropped his gaze. "I get soup, but you can't make it without water. It has nothing to do with you."

He really could be almost adorable.

She let the smile reach her lips as she took the bucket down. "Well, I won't deprive you of your soup."

"You better not. We have a deal—" He lifted his hands. "I mean a trade."

"Good man." She poured the water into the pot. "I'm glad you're learning."

"Hard not to," he grumbled.

"Are there any ingredients that would definitely help restore your magic? Anything else you've thought of?"

Wincing, he shrugged. "I never really did the cooking for that. Just the eating. So I don't know."

"Well...we'll find the answer soon, I'm sure. It's going to be a little later tonight before it's done. I got distracted. I'm sorry about that."

He grunted in response and started to lean on the windowsill, then pulled back. "It happens. What were you reading?"

"I was reading about food and magic. Can blood fae smell the magic of other races?"

Shrugging, he crinkled his nose as if testing the air. "Is there something I should be smelling?"

"No, I don't think so. I was just curious. You said you were unwanted last night. Is someone looking for you?"

He managed a small laugh as he braced his hands against his periwinkle sash. "Not with my luck."

"Is that good luck or bad?" She transferred the soaked beans to the pot.

His smile faded. "Bad these days. More or less. But it has its benefits. If no one is looking for you, no one can find you, good or bad. And that's good ultimately. So you could say my luck is actually good then."

He didn't sound convinced.

She set the cast iron skillet on the stovetop and placed three strips of bacon in it. Whoever Traelan was looking for—whatever reason Traelan was looking for a blood fae—it couldn't be Ryul. Despite his fine clothes and beautiful lavender hair, he looked almost dejected out there. Practically harmless despite his size. He didn't even have prominent fangs. Or really any at all. Not that she could see.

That was strange.

She sliced up the onion, mulling this over. "Do you like traveling alone then?"

"I don't usually. But…for now, it is what it is. After my magic is restored, I won't have to worry about it. Though…" His brow knit with further consternation.

"Though what?"

He shook his head. "It's nothing. Just—I don't know that even if my magic is restored whether I will know what to do. What the next step is."

"The next step for what?"

Finding his family maybe? She stopped short of asking that, not wanting to wound him.

He remained silent, his gaze fixed on the ground.

"Everything," he mumbled. Sighing, he shook his head. "But for now, soup. What kind did you say you were making tonight? Something with beans?"

"White bean with pork and thyme. It has garlic in it too. And I'll add some other spices for good measure."

"How did Buttons do today?"

"Very well. He's quiet when there are customers, so I don't have to worry about him drawing attention. And he doesn't seem to mind the heat. Would you like something to drink? I can offer you water or milk."

"I'm all right." He managed a small but crooked smile. "Your day was good then?"

"Good enough." She almost laughed. Were they really just going to talk about their days? Maybe that wasn't a terrible thing. "What about yours?"

"Hmmm. Can't leave during the day, so it is what it is. Do you really like making soup? I imagine you meet a lot of people out here."

"A fair number," she said. Turning, she picked up a stool and passed it to him through the window. "Here. You can sit on this if you want to. Or, if you don't want to, set it aside. Either way. Doesn't matter to me."

He took it, set it down, and then sat on it gingerly. "Thank you." A pause followed. Then, he cleared his throat. "Would you tell me about your day?"

"It isn't particularly interesting."

He shrugged but continued to watch her, his amethyst eyes far softer now.

"Fine." She sighed. "I suppose we could talk about something. Even though my days are really just a whole lot of nothing."

She launched into a full account of her morning and all the chores and tasks, and he listened with very little commentary, his gaze fixed on her as if it really wasn't the most boring thing he had ever heard in all his life.

THE DANGERS WITH BLOOD FAE

It was hard for Erryn to fathom that anything she had to say could be that interesting, but Ryul continued to listen, occasionally asking questions about soup and cooking and people. Especially whether people around here were friendly or if they disliked strangers and whether a lot of people came through. Boring him with the tedious details of her chores and practices all the way up to the noon hour did not appear to dissuade him at all. She didn't tell him past that.

And when it was time to eat, he insisted again that she join him. She pulled her own stool up near the window, though she still wasn't close enough for him to reach through. It was a little awkward to sit on a backless stool with no table in front of her and eat soup. But she balanced herself carefully, with one foot hooked over the stool's rung as she took a bite. The soft white beans, rich pork broth, and pungent thyme reminded her of autumn festivals and all the different bean soups. Warmth spread through her, bittersweet and strong.

As she glanced up, she realized he was watching her. Then he smiled. The warmth spread a little faster. Her gaze dropped back down to the savory dish cradled in her hand, her palm protected by the thick bottom.

"It's good," he said.

"Good." She took another bite, savoring it and focusing on the smooth texture of the beans. It actually was. What made it nicer was being able to share a meal with someone. "Is this fixing your magic?"

"Can't tell." He shoveled a couple more bites. "Still good, regardless."

By the time she finished her one bowl of soup, he finished the rest of the pot and then fetched her more water so she could wash it out. She scoured and cleaned it as he asked more questions about soup making and where she got her recipes. Nothing important. But still pleasant.

Buttons ran between the window and the sink or counter, sometimes barking and sometimes dancing about as he begged for scritches and belly rubs.

Then an hour or so before dawn, he left. This time, Ryul bid her and Buttons good night and promised to return the following night.

When she crawled into bed, she found it a little harder to drift asleep despite her exhaustion. Was it just a game to him? Was he just toying with her?

Maybe.

You really couldn't rule that out with strangers.

The following day started with a lighter haze and slightly cooler weather. She spent more time out in the grass with Buttons, playing fetch and running alongside him. He leaped and jumped, sometimes straight into the air, his wings twitching.

"Are you trying to fly, baby boy?" she asked.

He barked and leaped again.

Sweeping didn't get done. Neither did shaking the rugs and a few other chores, but she set to the chopping and prepping. Soon, the kitchen steamed with heat and savory scents, banishing all traces of the morning's relative coolness.

Today required an extra pot of summer bounty because Eddie was coming to pick up the whole pot for her shut-in tour. In winter, she'd take two. Erryn didn't even bother to dish up the soup for that order. She just used the dented old pot that Eddie had given her back at the start, and they swapped pots for the week.

Traelan stopped in, earlier in the afternoon this time but after the midday rush. "I'll have some of that bean soup you were making yesterday," he said a little too cheerily as he rubbed his hands together briskly.

"Oh, I already sold it all." She avoided scowling or rolling her eyes as she picked up the wooden spoon and gestured to the biggest pot of simmering goodness. "But I've got extra vegetable. That's what you wanted yesterday, right?"

He chuckled, hands now braced against his silver belt. "Seems odd you sold out of it so fast. And there isn't even a dirty pot."

"Are you offering to help me wash the dishes? Very

kind of you, but it's all right. I took care of everything." She gestured to the line of clean pots on the back counter. "So…vegetable, chicken, or summer bounty?"

"My, my, you are efficient. Summer bounty and vegetable."

"Mixed or separate?"

"Surprise me."

She dished it up into two containers and set them on the counter beside him. "Best to keep it separate, I think."

He placed the coins next to them. His expression had grown more somber. "I apologize if I came on too strong yesterday. It's just that, in my travels, I have become concerned for those who might be harmed or taken advantage of. Blood fae can be so charming when they want something. It's hard to resist them. Even when one is intelligent and full of good sense."

"I don't think I have ever met a fae who wasn't charming when they wanted to be. Nor many other races for that matter. And I know there are good and bad among them all. Pretty tough to make a decision based on race." She glanced beyond him, hoping to see another customer.

Traelan chuckled. "You say that, and yet you use warding and charms."

"Yes." She crossed her arms. "I also use locks and bolts. I'm not the brightest, but I'm not the dumbest either. Ordinary locks and bolts don't work against some kinds of magic. So other measures are needed. If a blood fae or a lich strolled up and asked for some soup, I'd gladly serve them, but I'd stay in here where their magic would be kept back."

"Weakened. Not fully pushed back." He tilted his head. "That certainly wouldn't do much to nullify the offense of being treated so differently either. But you realize what is so insidious with so many like that is that their voices are often just enough. All they have to do is say the right words. In some cases, all it takes is you saying the right words. You know what happens if you tell a blood fae you love them, don't you?"

She stiffened, prickles of unease passing through her. "I do."

"No matter what they say, there are no limits on that wish. You say the words—and then—one wish—whatever they want. No matter what. Even your own life or the life of someone you love. And if you refuse to fulfill it, you bleed. From your mouth. From your eyes. More and more until you either fulfill it or you die. How many do you think have been tricked in such a manner and lost far too much in exchange?"

"Too many." She put the lids back on the pots. "But you needn't worry about me. I don't make deals or bargains with fae."

"Yet you sell soup to them."

"Those are trades, simple exchanges of goods. Believe me, I don't have to be convinced how dangerous an open-ended or ambiguous bargain can be."

"Hm." He frowned as he studied her. "You've been on the wrong side of a bargain before, haven't you?"

The lies about her past rose in her mouth, but she

stopped. Too dangerous. Too bitter to speak again here. Both lies and the truth were unwanted.

"Just leave it at I don't do bargains, and I am done with this conversation."

"Very well. I apologize once more for any discomfort or inconvenience I have caused, but if you—"

She held up her finger. "No. No more." She gestured to the doorway. "Have a good day, sir."

"You as well." He tipped his hat, then strode away, the pheasant feather bobbing with the movement.

She wanted to slam the door behind him, but she pulled the lid off the vegetable soup and began stirring again, scraping the wooden spoon along the bottom to ensure nothing burned. Her fingers tightened around the handle. Why must everything remind her of that cursed bargain? She'd been a fool to take it! She knew that.

And as for love...she shook her head. Even if blood fae weren't bound by such terrifying magical requirements, people like her weren't meant to have families again. And she could never risk trusting someone with her heart like that, especially not if it would give them total control over her for even a few moments. Really, that was utterly unfair given that they could already manipulate your blood and body like a marionette if you weren't properly protected.

Tonight, she planned to make potato soup. She carried on with her regular tasks of clean up and let Buttons out as soon as she could. The little dog greeted her with great enthusiasm. Her heart remained heavy, though. She wasn't the sort who fell in love, but her conscience tweaked at the thought of making Ryul continue to stand out there so uncomfortably. Not that she could let him in. But he had not done anything to threaten her or show any signs of doing harm, really. In fact, he'd been quite patient with her trying to figure out what soups would work.

A thought presented itself, small but hopefully kind. She pulled one of the shelves out of the cupboard and then clamped it to the outside of the windowsill. If he intended to spend another night chatting with her while the soup cooked, this would make it a little more comfortable without putting her in danger.

PLANKS AND MYTHS

Everything else went well. She swept up, diced potatoes, filled the water vessels, and made her preparations for the night. She should have been exhausted.

But she wasn't. A bit of excitement welled within her. Despite Traelan's words, she didn't fear Ryul's arrival. If anything, she felt some measure of protectiveness toward him. She didn't fully trust him. But you didn't need trust to want to protect someone or be kind to them, right?

As the sun went down, she had the potato soup cooking away. It was a little richer than what she usually made, using up the last of her butter and all of the remaining milk. Not that it mattered. She'd already marked down the extra ingredients she would need. Tomorrow morning, Darri would pick up her list and the coin when he brought the ice, and then he would fetch the necessary items from the city. He might raise an eyebrow at some of the added items. They *were* rather unusual, but as she was paying for them, it wouldn't make any difference. She never splurged on herself, so she did have enough to allow for a few odd items.

Ryul arrived shortly after dark as usual. "It smells good," he offered from outside the window.

"Always good to hear." She set the cast iron skillet on one of the burners. "It's potato soup tonight. I'm going to fry up some bacon to put on the top."

"Sounds good—" He stopped, tilting his head as he noticed the makeshift plank ledge. "What's this?"

"Hmmm? Nothing." She dusted her hands off. "Just thought it would be better there."

"I can…can I lean on it?"

"If you'd like." She pulled the brown packet of bacon out of the icebox.

His mouth pulled up a little as he rested his elbows against the wooden surface and peered in. Buttons barked at him, panting happily. "How was your day?"

"Nothing unusual. Yours?"

"There really can't be anything unusual for me." His hands clasped his elbows as he continued to survey the cottage with a curious gaze. "Night is when everything happens."

"Are all blood fae nocturnal? Your powers are influenced by the moon, I know, but I didn't think you were only able to go out at night."

"The moon's effects last no matter what the time of day or night. And we do whatever works best so far as being nocturnal or whatever the other is."

Conversation drifted to the moon and weather,

somehow far more pleasant than her conversations with the travelers and regulars despite being little more than mild chitchat. There was something about his voice. Something that soothed her. Especially when he talked in this lower calmer manner. With the bacon now frying, the soup cottage had taken on an even cozier feeling.

"So are you alone here all the time then?" Ryul rested his chin on his palm.

"More or less. It's nice and quiet."

And lonely at times. She bit that statement back.

"No spouse or lover?"

She huffed a small laugh as she picked up the tongs to turn the bacon. She took hold of the handle to turn the skillet. "No—oh, son of a walnut!"

Fiery pain seared through her palm. She shoved the cast iron skillet aside. It tipped. Hot grease poured out onto the black burner. Flames shot up. Dark smoke curled up from the burners. Buttons let out a frightened whimper followed by a sharp bark.

Ryul stiffened, then leaned up to the edge of the windowsill. "Erryn?! Are you all right?"

Her eyes burned as she started coughing. Stooping down, she grabbed up the clay pot of sand, shoved her hand in, and grabbed up a fistful. She cast it onto the flames as more smoke billowed up. Her eyes watered.

Buttons barked louder.

"Erryn?" Ryul called out.

She opened the door to let the smoke out faster. Buttons bolted out.

"Buttons!" she shouted, starting forward, then dissolving into more coughs.

The little dog was already halfway out to the tree, his wings tucked firmly against his back and his tongue lolling. He circled the tree and barked more, his stub of a tail wagging a little as he looked back at her.

"Buttons, get back here!"

She glanced up into the night sky and then at Ryul. If he decided to break the deal, he could. He could snatch Buttons up and run. He could even claim it wasn't a violation because none of her soups had done more than be basic nourishment.

"Buttons!" Erryn clapped her hands together, then dashed back to the stove to toss more sand on the stove to finish off the fire. It wasn't going to do any good if the whole house caught on fire, would it?

She ran back in time to see Buttons sniffing at Ryul's fingers. She grabbed for one of the skillets on the wall, ready to lunge out and attack if it looked like he was going to take him.

But something held her back.

Ryul said something too quiet for her to hear. Buttons licked at his hand, yipping happily.

"I won't hurt him," Ryul said without looking at her. "I would never hurt a real dog. Would prefer to not hurt a fake one either. And he's been a real one for a good bit now."

If Buttons' judgment was to be trusted, Ryul wasn't a threat at all. Her heart warmed a little. There was no reason for Ryul to carry on an illusion of caring, was there?

"Is the fire out?" Ryul scratched under Buttons' chin. "The smoke isn't as dark."

"Yeah. It's probably going to smoke for a while longer." She wiped her hand across her eyes, ducking away as more rolled out. The wind picked up as if to help usher it out. The soup looked to be relatively unscathed as well.

"I don't see any signs of night predators," he said. "There really haven't been many about lately. I can watch him out here. I've gotten good at watching for them anyway since I can only be out at night."

"What do you mean?" she frowned. She waved the towel again to boost the smoke's departure.

"Cursed. Can't set foot on the earth when the sunlight touches it." He shrugged as if this was just the way it was and nothing to be done about it.

"What?" She almost stepped over the threshold to better see him, still holding her burned hand to her chest. "You're cursed?"

"It happens. It wouldn't be quite so difficult, except, well..." He shook his head, his lips pressed into a tight line. Picking up a fallen stick, he gestured to Buttons. "Come on. You want to catch it? You want to catch the stick?" Buttons barked, crouching down, his stub of a tail wagging faster. "Go get it!" He tossed it.

Buttons raced after the coarse-barked branch and returned. When Ryul tried to take it back, he growled and tugged back.

"You'll have to let go if you want me to throw it again," Ryul said.

Another growling yip followed. Then Buttons

released the stick and bounded around. Ryul tossed it once more. He then glanced back at her, his smile soft.

Her stomach somersaulted as she returned the smile. "Make sure nothing happens to him then. I'll get the rest of this sorted."

His mouth quirked a little higher. "Don't worry. Nothing will happen to him." He took the stick back as Buttons dropped it at his feet and barked again.

She watched a moment longer then stepped back. Using a woven hot pad, she moved the still-hot cast iron skillet. The bacon was far too crispy now. But the fire was gone. Most of the smoke rolled out, the heavy scent lingering even though the door remained open.

She then tended the stove, cleaned up, and rebuilt the fire. The soup, at least, was unharmed. She had barely finished when Buttons ran into the cottage, his little black nails clicking on the wooden floor. Ryul had returned to the window.

"Thank you for taking care of him while he was out there." She pulled the blue-lidded jar of burn salve down from the cupboard and rubbed some in. "It sounded like he had fun."

"He did. He likes running. He'll probably like flying, too, if he ever gets up the strength for it."

"He'll be able to fly?"

He shrugged. "He's got wings. I've never seen one like him before, but I'd assume he could in time." His brow creased as his gaze dropped to her hand. "Let me see."

"Why?" She held her wrist to her chest, the salve still glistening on the reddened flesh.

He extended his own and then traced a line from his wrist up over his palm. Red light flared briefly, following the path of the blood vessels. "It will help carry the salve's healing through your veins. It won't heal you completely, but it will help it heal faster."

She hesitated, then complied, reaching through the window. He cradled the back of her hand as he studied her palm. A shiver spiraled through her as her insides tightened.

Following the same movement he demonstrated on his own, he made a line up and across. His touch was surprisingly gentle. The burn flared in color along with the blood vessels, but her discomfort eased almost at once.

He stroked the side of her hand with his thumb. "Is that better?"

She nodded. "Thank you." Her gaze met his. That tightening within her reached her breaths. She cleared her throat, heat flaring into her cheeks. "I'm sorry there won't be any bacon for crumbles, but the potato soup is done. Just a little smoky maybe. Do you still want some?"

"As long as you're all right."

"I'm..." She started to say good, surprised to realize she did in fact feel good. Even with the burn. Not neutral. Not fine. Not adequate. Some bit of happiness bubbled inside her. "Yes." She drew her hand back. "Yes, we could both use some soup, I think."

His gaze followed her as she moved back to the broad stove, though she tried to pretend she didn't notice. She dished up two large bowls of the creamy potato soup and topped them with chives. Then she placed both on the windowsill and plank. As she pulled up a stool, his eyes widened.

"You're not—"

"Did you think I only set up this plank for you?" She tried to sound casual as she picked up her spoon with her left hand. It was a little awkward to use this hand, so, of course, she had to focus on that.

A slow smile spread over his pleasant mouth. He adjusted his stool as well. "Well, that's good. I'd rather you didn't go out of your way for me. Unless it's for something that would benefit you too."

They ate in silence for a few minutes longer. Then she blurted out her own question. "Why did you tell me not to fall in love with you that first night? Did you think I would just because I'm a human? Because I'm a woman?"

"Hmmm?" His eyebrows lifted. A faint look of alarm passed over his tanned face. "No. I just—it would be awkward if you did. We have—blood fae, I mean—if someone tells us they love us—"

"I know about that."

It was a horrible magical requirement too.

He winced. "It's a big responsibility. Very easy to make bad or have something unintended happen. It tests the heart and tempts us."

She almost laughed. "You worry about that? Try worrying about being the person who is vulnerable to it."

"There's this myth I always liked." He tapped his fingers on the clay cup and then picked it up. "Omat and Huldah. Some details change depending on who tells the story, but my favorite version was the one where they were a weaver and a healer, and they initially fought over who should get to use a certain plant. But there are many stories about them. The adventures they went on. The sights that they saw. The way that they changed and defined the way that blood fae could interact with others. The wish was a great concern though. But when she confessed to him that she loved him, he wished for her happiness and fulfillment in her pursuits and promised to love her fully forever by blood and by soul and by will. Forever."

"Very romantic." She stirred her soup. "I see why it's a beloved myth."

"There's always a risk of a wish being twisted or corrupted. And the receiver of the wish will face enormous temptation in that moment. But they say that if the one who receives the wish truly loves the one who gives it, then it will be true and simple, and they will not give in to the temptation. It's the twisting of the one who receives it that can make it go bad."

"All the more reason to consider it exceptionally dangerous and ill-advised. There's no way of knowing whether someone is really telling you the truth."

He nodded slowly, turning the clay cup in his hand. "And how do you really know if you mean something? You can think you mean it and then later realize you don't or that there were other things you wanted more. It's terrifying. To know that you could ruin someone's life like that is a lot to consider."

She almost laughed. It had never occurred to her

that a blood fae would find that particular tradition or requirement troubling.

"Then why not keep it simple then? Wish for a daisy. Or a cup of coffee."

"If someone tells you that they love you, they are giving you a great gift. The wish must recognize that worth. Otherwise, it's an insult. It has to be beautiful. Otherwise, you're inviting more curses on yourself and your union. Besides, no matter what the wish, it tests your heart and what you really feel against what you want. What makes it harder is that when a wish like that is freely given, it is filled with great power. There's a chance that no matter what you ask for—even if it is more than what the giver can provide—it will be granted because all the heavens and all the magic and all the good of all will come together to make it so. Whether that's true or just part of the temptation, I don't know. You always have to be on guard against the curses, though."

"More curses?" She raised an eyebrow at this. That was a part she hadn't heard before.

"It's part of being fae. Navigating all of the magic. Part of being a blood fae, in particular. Not that I know what it is to be any other type. And there is still much for me to learn. Everyone encounters it a little differently too." He finished the last bite in his bowl. "Is there more soup?"

She smiled as she took his bowl. "Plenty."

THE STORM

The next few days passed calmly and ordinarily. Erryn continued to hide Buttons, and she took down the plank each morning so that no one would notice it. Darri commented both on the increased number of unusual items as well as the smell of smoke. But he still completed all his tasks, including laying up more wood for her and ensuring she had all the items from her list.

Traelan returned but only purchased soup and implied he might be going on an intriguing quest. She asked no questions but bid him well. When he returned the following day, she followed the same pattern. Of all the people she had met recently, he was the one most likely to have some answer about blood fae magic, but she couldn't risk it.

Ryul returned each night, and each night, she let him take Buttons out to play. More than once, she caught him holding the little dog and talking to him in quiet tones. Any residual concerns she might have had about him harming the pup faded entirely. Especially once he started trying to teach Buttons how to fly and crouched down on the ground beside him. Where were his wings though? Didn't all fae have wings? Unless there was some horrific accident, of course.

Probably best not to ask.

They both sat at the windowsill and ledge, enjoying the soups: chicken noodle, black bean surprise, green soup, and mushroom leek. Ryul grew almost apologetic in acknowledging that the soup wasn't healing his magic, but he told her not to worry about it. Their trade was just for soup that she tried to make to restore his magic. And he liked her soup a great deal.

Nan arrived two days later. A normal occurrence at the middle of the month. She walked with a slower tread this time, leaning more heavily on her bulbous wooden cane. In the early days, she had come to supervise and ensure Erryn had everything she needed. Now the visits were more social than anything.

"You seem to be doing even better than before," Nan observed as Erryn put a steaming mug of tea on the counter before her. "There's a happy sort of light in your eyes."

"It's the change in the seasons. I love autumn."

Not entirely a lie. But she had been smiling a lot more lately. Even when sweeping or washing dishes or cleaning up little messes that Buttons made.

"Hmmm. Is that it?" Nan chuckled as she wrapped her hands around the thick mug. "I almost thought perhaps you had met someone."

"I meet lots of people here." Erryn took a demure sip of her own black tea.

Ryul's face at once sprang into her mind, his warm amethyst eyes and that clever smile and the gentle way he spoke when he was contemplating something. She stiffened. No, that was—that wasn't anything she meant to focus on. It wasn't wise anyway. He was a blood fae. She would never ever make a bargain with a fae like the one that would be triggered if she ever admitted she was in love. Besides, falling in love was not for someone like her.

"True." Nan nodded slowly. "And one day, perhaps you will meet someone who will want to whisk you away."

"I'm not going anywhere any time soon."

Nan smiled a little, a hint of sadness in her eyes. "Taking a chance on love does have its risks. Another of my granddaughters is finding the sorrowful side of that, I fear. More than one, actually. But she's had it the worst, I think. She has the worst luck in love of any girl I've known."

"Something happened to Ina?"

Ina always seemed to be the one in the most obvious trouble, and the one Erryn guessed would be most likely to replace her here. Except that the young woman utterly despised the thought of working in a soup cottage. Besides, whenever there was a problem with one of the grandchildren, Nan and Loto swept in. She'd gotten used to hearing about various crises over the years, some of which resulted in significant expenditures and both Nan and Loto being in Moro for weeks and weeks at a time.

Nan took a long sip of her tea and clicked her tongue. "Well, her heart was broken. Poor girl. Loto and I will be going to see her soon. Her and all them in the city."

"Should I plan on looking for a new home?" Her stomach clenched, the brightness fading within her.

"No," she said slowly. "You'd be welcome to stay here until after winter regardless. But if it becomes necessary, we've told Ina she can come back here. She'd need to stay here because we've got the others at our house until they recover. Marcus and Teino and the little ones. And we're still taking care of Auntie Plum. So our house is all but bursting. In the meantime, perhaps you should keep the coin you make from this place."

"Are you sure you'll be all right without the coin?" Erryn frowned.

"We'll be fine, dear." Nan patted her hand. "It's not money that's the issue these days. It's space and making sure you find everyone you need and keeping them out of trouble. There's so much temptation in Moro. But they've held fast. So proud of them. All of them. But I'm worried about Ina. She might not be able to resist all the lures and bargains and magic with her heart like this. Best we can do is offer her a place to come back to. So you keep the profits for at least the next month."

"And if Ina or the others don't want to come here after a month, I can pay you the difference afterward."

Nan shrugged, smiling warmly. Her cornflower-blue shawl bunched with the movement, and affection shone in her eyes. "It's been a good year in most respects. Consider this a gift. You're still covering the costs of ingredients and supplies and such, so it isn't as if this will cost us more. We can manage with what we're getting elsewhere. You've done an excellent job with the soup cottage, Erryn. Better than any of us ever hoped."

"I appreciate you giving me the opportunity to do something here." She slowed her breaths, fighting to keep the panicked thoughts from upending her. Nothing was certain yet. And she'd always known that this was temporary. If Ina moved in, she could manage. Though how would she explain Buttons? Or Ryul, for that matter.

"I am certain that no matter what comes, your future will be bright." Nan took another sip from her tea. "Did you hear they are building a new theater in Moro?"

"No."

"It sounds as if it will be quite lovely. All the girls are looking to get involved. I haven't seen Lysa or Seren for months now, even though we visited three weeks ago. They're all so busy these days. Living such bold beautiful lives. I'm proud of all of them, though I miss them. It'll be hard for Ina to leave them behind in all the glamor of the city, but I hope that she'll see reason if that is what's best."

Nan spoke lightly about the different things she had heard about Moro and how city life differed from life on the edge of the Barrens Wild and even in their small town. She spoke proudly of each of her grandchildren in turn, recounting their adventures. Most of which she only heard second or third-hand. Pride shone in her dark-blue eyes and made the fine wrinkles along her brows and eyes all the deeper.

When she finally left, she squeezed Erryn's hand again and promised her everything would work out. "Ina's a sweetheart. If you two do have to share space for a time, I know you'll be the absolute best of friends."

Erryn bid her farewell and thanked her.

After setting the tea mugs aside, she hugged herself tight. She had been beyond lucky, blessed, and fortune-kissed to find a place such as this. With summer essentially over, she did have time. Not much, but some. She had some coin, enough that she could last for a time, though she'd need to be careful with how much she spent on extras.

What was next though? What could she do?

She still hadn't figured out the perfect soup recipe for Ryul.

She set her hands against the slab counter and let her gaze drift around the cottage. Precious little here was actually hers. She could probably pack it all away in a single rucksack. Even if she packed that one special dress. The one indulgence she'd allowed herself in all these years.

No one else came for the rest of the day. Heavy clouds gathered on the horizon, darkening the sky before dusk and requiring her to light candles and lamps earlier than usual.

Buttons scratched at the door and whined earlier as

well. As there was no one else coming until Ryul arrived, she let him out early, put the plank back up, and tried to find some additional scrap of knowledge in the books that would guide her in restoring Ryul's magic.

The cottage still smelled a little of the greasy smoke, but the scents of the soup covered up most everything else. As for what she would prepare tonight, perhaps a chicken summer bounty with something from all of the harvest? She chewed on the inside of her lip.

"Everything all right?"

His voice washed over her, startling and yet almost comforting her at the same time.

Peering up from the book, she tried to smile. "Just thinking about things. I haven't been able to get the recipes right."

Ryul leaned on the plank, that small smile curling at his lips. "You're doing your best."

She really didn't deserve him being that understanding about it. Sighing, she shook her head and forced her gaze back to the page. How much longer could she really carry this on though? And if she lost the soup cottage and hadn't found a solution—

Thunder growled in the distance.

He glanced back into the sky, his brow furrowing.

That storm was going to be a big one. Especially with how hot it had been recently. The overhang beyond the window would not shield him much.

"Would you like to join me in here?" she asked.

Her stomach tightened, but she brushed the fear

aside. If he was going to be dangerous, he had had ample opportunities already.

He froze, then turned his head, his amethyst eyes wide. "You said I could—I can come in?"

"If you want. It's going to storm."

More thunder grumbled as if in agreement. Lightning flashed in the dark clouds as he moved from the window to the door.

Her heart beat a little faster, her hands sweating. This might be the most foolish thing she'd done.

But she didn't care about that any more.

She picked up a green vial of marking oil and made a sign on the door, then opened it. He stood on the other side, still eyeing her with caution. "Give me your hand," she said.

He hesitated, then obeyed, turning his palm up. "You're sure?"

With swift strokes, she marked the symbol across his hand in a fluid motion. "I'm sure. Come inside before you get struck by lightning or worse."

He ducked his head to avoid the low beam of the doorjamb and then crossed over the threshold with an almost tentative glance at her as if to ensure she really meant this.

She nodded. Heat coiled within her. Why? It was just a simple act of kindness.

After setting the oil aside, she picked up one of the radishes for the night's soup, focusing on its bright coloration and the bit of green at the top. It had been a good year for radishes.

Buttons barked and scampered about. He jumped

up on his hind legs and practically danced. Ryul smiled a little as he stooped and rubbed the dog's short folded ears.

Buttons lapped at Ryul's hand and nuzzled him.

Ryul whispered as if there was some chance she might not hear him. "Oh, yes, such a good one, aren't you? Not a garm, but such a good boy." As he continued to scratch Buttons' ears, he glanced around. "You're getting low on supplies, aren't you? Or do you have another store room?"

"Oh." His observation startled her. Before she could concoct a lie, the truth slipped out. "No. They're just getting low."

She was going through supplies faster than usual.

"It's almost autumn though. Are you planning on returning to the city for winter? Or will you start preparing soon?" He stood. Somehow, the concern that radiated from his pinched expression seemed...sincere.

She trimmed the tops from the radishes and dropped them into the bowl for composting. It was suddenly a more painful question than it should have been.

"I'll be fine. I always am. And I'm very aware of my situation."

He strode around the cottage, brow still furrowed and hands on his trim waist as he took it all in. "There is a big difference here now compared to what it was —" He turned to face her, his eyes widening. "I'm eating all your supplies, aren't I?"

"We made a trade," she said evenly. Not that she had expected him to devour the entire pot of soup each night. This blood fae could eat for twelve. "If I went to the city and bought a dog, do you think they would let me pay in soup? Of course not. So don't worry about it."

His brow smoothed. "The only reason they wouldn't is because they haven't tried your soup."

"My very non-magical soup." She tossed him a head of garlic. "Make yourself useful and start peeling."

"Hmmm." He wrinkled his nose. "Garlic skin is... like paper you can't get off your fingers."

"Now you know why I don't like to peel it. Unfortunately, it's an integral ingredient to most of the recipes I know. Both healing and pleasurable."

"Pleasurable?" He raised an eyebrow, a smile quirking up. "I don't think they put garlic in the passion chocolates or the love cakes."

She wrinkled her nose at him in response. "I mean, eating for pleasure. Not eating for—whatever it is you'd be doing if you're eating love cakes."

"Not peeling garlic." He chuckled. He scrunched his face still further as he held up his hand with a few errant strips of garlic peel still clinging to it. "Garlic is the least attractive vegetable that ever existed."

"You certainly shouldn't be eating it right before you kiss anyone. Or right after. Or maybe not even a few hours after. But it tastes good, and it is good for you."

"I just want to crush it."

"Well, don't. It needs to be minced."

"No one is going to know if it's minced or crushed," he said coyly. "We could break the rules."

"Listen to me very carefully, blood fae. It is my soup recipe. If I say the garlic must be minced, it shall be minced. Or I'll be adding blood fae blood to it." She pointed with the knife, speaking with mock severity.

"I don't think that's a good ingredient for any soup." He continued to peel the garlic and then set the cloves of garlic on the counter. "Do you tease me because you like me, Erryn?"

Her grip on the knife nearly slipped, the blade nicking dangerously close to her fingers. "What?"

He picked up another clove. "In my family, we tease people we like. It's a way of showing that they mean something to us. And it's good to laugh. But some people tease because they do not like them. And I am curious."

She bit the inside of her lip. Her stomach twisted. It was hard to force the words out amid the flutters, and the soft but frank way he asked made her heart beat even faster.

"I tease you because I like you."

"Good." He peeled away more of the garlic skin and set it down. "Because I like you. Quite a lot. And I am not really certain how to tease you. Or what to do around you."

Her cheeks heated. "Oh."

"Did I just make you uncomfortable?" he asked.

"No, it's just—well—" She cleared her throat. "I just—"

"I know I told you that you shouldn't fall in love with me. Dared you not to, I suppose. And I know that it has to be unnerving because of what the magic would do, but—"

"It won't happen." She forced a smile and steeled herself as she looked back into his eyes.

He didn't flinch, though his brow did tweak. "Won't happen because..."

"Because I don't make bargains—especially not ones with open ends—and because we haven't known each other long enough to know anything about one another and also because I wouldn't be any good for you."

"Why wouldn't you be any good for me?"

She chopped faster, but she shook her head. This wasn't something she wanted to think about. Especially not now.

"Just trust me on that, all right?"

Aside from the storm's growls and the steady downpour of the rain on the roof, silence descended. More so than usual. An uncomfortable silence. At least that was how it seemed at first.

Then she noticed he wasn't actually acting out of sorts about it. He finished peeling the garlic, then helped her dice the tomatoes and chop the onions. His expression had grown contemplative, but there was no resentment. At least none that she could see.

By the time the soup finished simmering, quiet conversation had returned. Not about anything in particular. The storm. The night. The changing of the seasons.

This time, they both sat next to one another at the round wooden table and shared the chicken and summer bounty soup. When they finished, they washed and dried the dishes together. He even swept the floor and gathered up all the thin bits of garlic paper that had escaped and playfully threatened to put it in her tea. She laughed, of course, and promised him far worse if he ever should.

The rain had let up and the clouds passed by the time he was ready to leave. When he reached the door, he held it open and hesitated at the threshold. "I don't agree with you that you would not be good for me. And I understand why the magic would make this far more unnerving. But I want you to know that I do cherish our friendship. I am glad to have met you, Erryn. Even if I don't know how to tease you well. You're a kind person, and your soup is excellent."

She wrapped her arms around herself and smiled. "I'm sure that given enough time, you'll figure something out. I probably just knocked your teasing abilities loose when I hit you with that skillet."

"It was rather heavy." He rubbed the side of his head as if remembering.

"I suppose that it's true what they say about iron being a fae's weakness."

His mouth screwed up, then he shook his head. "Any heavy blunt object to the head would have a similar effect. It bypasses all the defense mechanisms. You'll need to modify your expectations in future conflicts."

"Should I expect to have more conflicts with blood fae?"

"Not if I have anything to do with it." He smiled,

then stooped down to pet Buttons once more. "I hope it's a good day for you."

"I hope it is for you as well." She hugged herself as she walked to the door. "And you're welcome to come back in tomorrow night when you return. The door will be unlocked."

His smile broadened, his eyes brightening. He stood a little taller. "I'll see you soon, Erryn."

DISCOVERED

The way that fae could make her heart clench and her insides somersault and twist wasn't something she wanted to contemplate. It was just a crush. Nothing more.

And if those feelings tried to become something more, she would have to ignore them or grind them out of existence.

Even so, Erryn found it hard to sleep.

Buttons curled up next to her, his head on her shoulder and his body tucked in her arm. He licked her cheek.

"I suppose you like him now," she said softly.

He wagged his tail.

Fae were charming. And dogs were supposed to be excellent judges of character. Did fae charm extend to them? Could they be fooled?

She closed her eyes, but that soft way Ryul had smiled at her and that look of surprise and then delight when she had invited him in sent her pulse racing once more. Draping her elbow over her face, she released a long slow breath.

Morning came swiftly. Even with only a couple hours sleep, she found herself surprisingly full of energy. Maybe it was because she hadn't had to do cleanup on her own. Even the floor was already swept and the rugs straightened. He was surprisingly good at household chores.

Maybe that was the real reason she was feeling all gooey and soft. When she'd traveled on the road, the men she'd traveled with had simply expected her to handle most of the housekeeping tasks unless she'd asked for help. Ryul had volunteered to do it.

Glittering droplets of dew clung to the grass when she took Buttons out to play. After last night's storm, it had turned far cooler than in previous days. Autumn's chill had started to set in. The air smelled of wet earth, fallen leaves, and a hint of smoke from the hearths of the town homes some distance away.

Buttons bounded through the short grass, chasing butterflies, snapping at craneflies, and barking at tufts of tall grass. When a rabbit scurried out, he yip-shrieked, raced behind her, and barked even harder.

Laughing, she stooped down to pet him. "Are you afraid of the bunny, darling?"

"It certainly doesn't look like he should be."

Her muscles clenched, her heart leaping with fear.

Traelan.

What was he doing here so early?

Stuffing down the fear, she turned toward his voice. The red-cloaked man stood only a few feet away as if he had come from the Barrens Wild. But how? She hadn't heard even a footstep. Maybe she'd been too absorbed in watching Buttons.

"What are you doing out so early?" she asked with forced cheer. "Are you hunting for more artifacts and runes?"

He rested his hands on his belt as he strode closer. "That's a very interesting dog you have there. I don't remember you mentioning you had one."

"He stays in the bedroom while I have customers. Too many new people overexcite him." She picked Buttons up and stood, moving back toward the cottage. Despite the warmth of the sunlight on her face, she now felt cold.

"Where did you get him?"

Her chest tightened. She hated lying, even when it was necessary. She had to sell this one better than any other she had ever told.

"Sometimes, I go out past the boundary markers to look for ingredients for the soup. And I found this little darling." She gestured toward Buttons.

Despite the wings folded against his back and his dark-red eyes, he looked like a relatively ordinary, albeit not very bright, dog.

Traelan tilted his head. "So you just found him in the wilds?"

She nodded, forcing a big smile. "Exactly."

"You realize this dog is magical. It was formed from magic. Blood fae magic."

"Really?" She lifted her brows, staring at him wide-eyed. "I mean, I know he isn't totally ordinary. He does have wings after all. And the cutest little tuskies. But he isn't really that odd. There are so many strange things out there."

"And you just found him?" He stepped closer, his bright-green eyes narrowing.

"He came running to me." She kissed Buttons on the top of the head once more. He started wagging his tail faster, panting. "Sweet boy. All he needed was a home."

"And when did this happen?"

"Hmmm." She frowned, hugging the little dog closer. "Maybe a week or two ago. About ten days? I can't remember exactly. The days blur together. But it's like I already told you. I can't smell blood fae magic. Most humans can't smell magic at all unless it's very intense. This dog smells like a dog to me. Maybe a bit like chestnuts? Now you say that he isn't a dog, but should I believe you or my eyes?" She shrugged dramatically.

"No. He is a dog. Now. But he was made with magic." Traelan canted his head, his thick brown curls sliding over his shoulder. The hardness in his gaze remained. "And you don't know the blood fae who created him?"

"I didn't see him being created, no. He just ran up to me, and he is happy to stay with me. Probably because I feed him and give him a place to sleep." She kissed him between the eyes.

"Easy to see why he would want to stay. For now."

Her skin crawled. Her stomach was a pit of anxious energy. "So what are you doing here so early?"

"I was just out for a stroll," he said. That smile was no longer so pleasant, his eyes harder, evaluating her.

"Did you enjoy it? Most people don't venture out this way so early. Night is still a little too close for comfort. Especially if you're coming from the Barrens Wild."

His smile smoothed. "I always enjoy walking. If you would care to join me, I can show you some of the more fascinating finds. You can bring your dog, if you like."

"Maybe. Though I can't stay out long. I've got to get the soups started. The broths are still simmering, so I don't like to be gone long. It's almost time for me to start adding the other ingredients actually."

"Well," he said, his tone amiable enough despite the sharpness in his gaze. "If you change your mind, I'm almost always about."

"Hmmm, well, if I do change my mind, I'll be certain to tell you."

She turned and strode away, keeping her pace slow and focused as if nothing was wrong. All she wanted to do was run. It felt like he was still watching her, but she didn't dare glance back.

Polph! Had he bought the story?

He was suspicious about something, but what? What could he possibly think? Had she given anything away?

It was hard for her to focus on the rest of her tasks. Something wasn't adding up. Aside from their initial encounter, Ryul had shown no signs of being dangerous or even mildly threatening. Was it possible that Traelan was searching for him for some legitimate reason? Or was he just looking for blood fae in general? They could be dangerous and problematic, especially when in large groups.

Time passed slower this day. A fact made all the worse because fewer customers came by to pick up soup. Traelan arrived again a little after midday and purchased a container of summer bounty. He made no reference to Buttons, but he did tip his hat and wish her a good afternoon.

Unlikely.

She watched him leave.

What was he up to?

Her stomach twisted.

Buttons appeared unaware of any tension or concern. He pranced and played in the late afternoon, caught a few leaves, and barked at the grass even though there were neither squirrels nor rabbits about. Once he'd tired out, she took him back in and tried to calm her thoughts.

Impossible.

She paced, opening the door and peering out. Where was Ryul? He had never missed a night before.

Was this because of Traelan?

She'd half-expected Traelan to show up at dusk as well. Not that he had any reason to assume that a blood fae would be here tonight, right? Most blood fae weren't only nocturnal.

Scratching her arm, she peered out once more. She hadn't seen him outside when she had taken Buttons out.

Not unless he had hidden himself and lay in wait somewhere, but why would he?

No. This was just paranoia.

She hugged herself. Anyone who wore a red cloak wouldn't blend in easily.

Unless he had changed his clothes. And he had practically snuck up on her this morning.

Tonight. she'd just make a vegetable soup with noodles. She could fry up the last three strips of bacon as well for some added flavor.

It didn't take long to get everything prepared. The bacon sizzled on the stovetop.

Footsteps outside the door. Buttons' ears pricked forward. He let out an excited yip and charged to it. The door scraped open, and Ryul poked his head in. "I guess he heard me coming."

She smiled, relief flooding her. "You're a lot later than usual."

He stepped inside, holding a large bag in one hand and a raw but cleaned duck in the other. "Yes, well, it took me longer to figure things out. And after I caught and cleaned the duck, I realized I probably should have waited to do that here." He placed both on the counter. "These are for you."

She looked from the ingredients to him. "Where did you get all this?"

"I found it," he said with a far too casual shrug to be truly casual. She tilted her head, meeting his gaze with a questioning look until he sighed. "In my larder, all right?"

"Including the duck?" She bit back a laugh, so happy to see him she was near to bursting.

He huffed at her. "Fine. I found it after I hunted and prepared it."

So that was why he had been so late. Thank all the good that was out there it wasn't because of Traelan.

"That's very sweet of you, but I have to ask…why?"

His face reddened, especially over his sharp cheekbones and up over his brow. "I didn't think about where you were going to get the ingredients for the soup. And—well—I have ingredients. So use them." He gestured toward them and then shook his hands.

"This helps a lot." She shook her head. "I could just hug you, Ryul."

He scoffed as he rubbed the back of his neck. "I wouldn't refuse a hug."

She'd been half joking. But before she gave it more thought, she stepped out from behind the wooden countertop and crossed over to him. An awkward intensity built within her stomach and chest as if she were about to step onto a stage. Reaching him, she lifted up on the balls of her feet and put her arms around his neck.

"Thank you."

He hesitated only a breath before he returned the hug, gripping her startlingly tight. His breaths were sharp, his heart thundering faster against hers. An odd sound rose in his throat.

"Are you all right?" She tilted her head back to try to see him.

He held her closer. "It's been a long time since someone hugged me."

Her heart swelled as she rested her head on his shoulder. It felt so good to be in someone's arms again, clasped tight and held fast. It'd been a long time since anyone had hugged her like this. Or really at all.

This was a perfect moment. A moment she wanted to stop and cherish. Her eyelids slid shut.

The door slammed open, cracking against the wall and shaking the building. Traelan sprang inside, brandishing a silver sword. "Surrender now, answer my questions, and maybe I let you live."

Ryul shoved her behind him. Massive but nearly transparent wings erupted from his back, filling the cottage with the strong scent of smoke, iron, and cedar. They struck her in the face and knocked her back as he lunged between her and Traelan. One wing swept a shelf completely off the wall. The little jars shattered on the floor. They pulsed with startling power.

Polph. She cringed as the wings knocked her back a second time.

His trying to save her was almost more damaging than if Traelan had attacked her. She caught herself against the wall and pushed back up as Buttons cowered behind her.

"Who in the void are you?" Ryul snarled, glaring at Traelan. He'd spread his arms and broadened his stance, making himself seem larger, his fingers curled like claws. And fangs. He actually had fangs.

"Well." Traelan's brow tweaked as he lowered his

sword. "You're clearly not the one I'm looking for. Who are your parents, boy?"

"Who are you?" Ryul demanded. His fangs glistened especially bright at the tips, iridescent liquid gathering at the tips. Venom?

"Traelan, what are you doing here? You are not welcome here!" She tried to duck under Ryul's wing, but it pulsed and knocked her back again, muscles rippling along his back and spine. For looking like they weren't all there, they were startlingly strong.

Traelan did not take his gaze from Ryul's face. "I am looking for a particular blood fae. Wrongs must be righted, child. Who are your parents?"

"Are you a servant of Volsrei?" Ryul glared at him.

Traelan spat on the floor. "Death would be better."

"Hey!" She shoved Ryul's wing aside and stepped between him and Traelan. She snapped her fingers at Traelan. "Do not spit in my house. I don't care if you do have a sword. Also, there will be no fighting."

Ryul kept his gaze fixed on Traelan. "My parents were consumed in the fight against Volsrei."

"Who is your family?"

"The Blood Spear and the Red Thorn. My parents were Corvus and Elara. They were not the only ones claimed in the battle."

Traelan sheathed his sword. His manner softened. "Your family is an unusual one. I was sorry to hear of your loss. Is the rest of your family here?"

Ryul's face lined, a muscle in his jaw jumping. "No. I am alone."

Traelan set his arms akimbo, his brow furrowing.

He looked Ryul up and down, his gaze falling on his wings. "You're awfully young to be out of the family home, aren't you?"

"I'm two hundred seventy-eight," he said sourly, "and what I do is none of your concern. You're the one who broke in here."

"Only two hundred seventy-eight?" Traelan's dark eyebrows lifted. "That's very unusual."

What made that unusual? She scowled.

Ryul nodded, his focus still on Traelan. "I don't see how it is any of your concern."

"What happened to the rest of your family? If they are dedicated to the elimination of Volsrei, then—"

"Volsrei was defeated," Ryul said sharply.

"Truly?" Traelan frowned.

"I saw it with my own eyes. He was shattered across the realms."

"Is there a place where I might verify the truth of this matter?"

"Past boundary marker for the Barrens Wild and beyond the Raven Crag to the Eternal Pool. There are fragments scattered along with bits of his vessel. If you know what you're looking for, you're certain to find it."

Traelan looked him up and down as if contemplating something. "If that is so, then my family and my kind thanks yours."

"What family and what kind might that be?" Ryul demanded.

"I've intruded upon you enough for one night, I think." He put his hand to his hat and dipped his head forward. "My apologies for your loss." His gaze moved to Erryn. "And my apologies for the interruption."

She folded her arms tight across her chest. "It was very rude of you and unacceptable."

"It certainly was," he agreed. He turned to leave.

"Hey! Before you go, you clean that up." She pointed at the spit mark. "You do not spit on the floor in my house. It's bad enough that you barged in to begin with, but you spit on my floor and leave it? I do not think so."

Traelan gave her a hard look, shook his head, and chuckled. "Very well, good lady." He stooped down and wiped up the floor with the edge of his cloak. Then, with a flourish, he left. The door banged shut behind him, and the cool night breeze swept along through the windows as if to erase all traces.

MISSING FAMILY

"Are you all right?" Erryn locked the door as soon as it clicked shut.

Ryul stood there, translucent wings still flared and chest wide. As he breathed, he drew back as if starting to relax. "I'm fine." He halted, glancing around the interior of the cottage. "I'm so sorry. I've wrecked your home. Did I knock that into the soup?"

He pressed his hand to his mouth. When he pulled it away, his fangs had vanished.

She turned back to the stove. The pepper grinder from the shelf had somehow fallen in. Sweeping up the slotted spoon, she fished it out. "It'll clean up fine."

The spice jars and tea urn weren't going to be easily fixable, but that didn't matter.

"I'm still getting used to my wings," he admitted sheepishly. "I don't—I'll fix all this. I promise."

"Don't even worry about it."

There were far more important things. Especially if

she had to move, she wouldn't have been able to take those items with her, and they weren't sentimental.

"It's embarrassing, regardless," he muttered. "I'd rather no one see them like this. But...sometimes that's not possible to prevent. Especially if I'm alarmed. And I was afraid he might hurt you."

His wings had a decidedly unformed appearance to them. Faintly colored veins moved through them, their shape and form similar to a dragon's. Though they'd nearly knocked her over, they'd almost seemed to evaporate now. It was as if they were there and yet not. Maybe they were fading with his strength?

"They look almost like glass. Your wings, I mean."

"They're still developing. For someone like me, they'll—fluctuate, I suppose. They'll keep on developing until I'm around a thousand. So for now, they are just—well—inconvenient." He closed his eyes, a muscle pulsing along the side of his neck as he pulled the wings back in. Slowly, they folded against his back and then vanished.

"Can you fly then?"

"Not much better than Buttons for now. But he'll learn before I master it most likely. Especially with my magic depleted."

"About your magic." She put the fallen shelf back on the wall and picked up the broom to sweep up the fallen fragments. "The night we met, were you just coming out of battle against Volsrei? Whoever he is."

"No." Crouching, he gathered the larger pieces of broken pottery and set them aside. "That happened a long time ago." A heavy sigh rocked him. He massaged his brow. "No. I was—I've been trying to get back to my family. And I can't."

She wanted to ask what had happened. Her heart clenched. This was the first time he had spoken about his family. Neither of them had been especially open about their pasts.

Buttons sat in front of him and placed his paw on Ryul's knee.

He smiled a little, then tousled the dog's ears. "This little one was supposed to be a flying garm who breathed fire and opened pathways. That way, I could take what remained of my home and Quinn through whatever portal we fell through and be reunited with my siblings. I'd searched for so long to find the incantation and necessary pieces. It was a long shot. And my magic just isn't good enough to create something like that. It has changed. Even though the garm was supposed to be my..."

The disappointment in his words cut deep.

She gripped the broom handle a little tighter. He was alone. Maybe that was why she had felt that connection to him even without talking about this. She knew that loneliness.

"My magic wasn't strong enough to begin with. I didn't have as much as I should because of the battle."

"Against Volsrei?"

He nodded. "We won, though. My siblings. My cousins. All of us who were left. We shattered his consciousness and trapped pieces of it in different realms, putting it in stones and mortar to be built into structures. A tavern inn here. A flour mill there. That way, he'll never be able to come back together again. But our castle also broke apart, and their consciousness fractured. I think. I don't think all of it came with me."

"Your castle's consciousness?"

He placed another chunk of pottery on the table. "I don't even know how it happened, but it had to be something when we were finishing off Volsrei. All I know is that I found myself here. And the curse still lingered."

"The curse?"

This was all rather complicated and confusing.

He rubbed the back of his neck, his voice lower now. "None of us can touch the ground when the sunlight touches it." His shoulders sagged. "I don't think I'll ever find a way to fix even half of this, Erryn. It's beyond me. Buttons wouldn't have fixed it either. Quinn confirmed that. My magic is just too weak."

She moved to the stovetop and stirred the soup. Fragrant steam rose. The sharp smoky scents from Ryul's magic had faded. A heaviness weighed upon her.

"I'm so sorry. Also, dinner is going to be late tonight. Later than usual, I mean. I'm going to roast the duck and then add it to the soup. Do you need something to tide you over?"

"No. It'll work out." Though he said it with some cheer, it sounded forced. "I am learning more and more each day. And they're looking for me as well."

"And your magic is returning? Even though the soup isn't working?" Guilt built within her.

"It might be making it happen faster," he said. "It might just be that this is slow. And until I found you, I hadn't had good food. I don't actually know how to cook. The larder is usually full of raw ingredients. The magic of the castle handles that. I'll bring ingredients from now on."

She almost laughed. Of course he had a *magical* castle. Why wouldn't he? Not just an ordinary castle. No, it had to be magical.

She washed her hands in the basin and then set to scoring the duck with her slim paring knife. "Thank you again for the duck. I have a wonderful recipe for duck and noodles, but I don't know how to make it without the duck. I was just going to make noodles and vegetable soup for tonight with some of the dark broth, but this is far better."

He chuckled a bit as he rubbed his arm. "I suppose if it comes down to integral ingredients, duck is one of the most."

"Exactly." She flipped the duck over and scored the back with light even strokes. The way he looked at her made her heart melt. "And I'm glad that the soup is good for something. I'm just—I thought the books would have more information on how to restore your magic, and they don't, and I'm not sure who else to ask without rousing suspicion beyond those I've already asked. I haven't asked Traelan, but I'm not sure he'd help anyway. Maybe this will work. We haven't tried duck yet, and I've got some special spices I'll rub in."

"I don't think it will. It's just going to take time. It wasn't going to work the other way either." He gave Buttons an affectionate scratch. "My magic was never going to be enough."

"It was enough to make a really wonderful little dog." She closed the oven door and crossed over to him. "He's such a sweetheart. And you know, that makes me think there has to be something very special about your magic as well."

"Well, something." He smiled faintly. "But you know, I can only take credit for the initial form. The personality he has taken on is more a reflection of you."

"A little spastic. Afraid of rabbits. Devourer of dandelions and random weeds. You're right. That is me." She set her hands on her waist, hoping he would smile more. The sadness hanging over him weighed on her as well. "I just—I know that we didn't get started right, and not that I want to create another trade or bargain, but if I can help, I want to."

"Having somewhere to go has helped, and having food that tastes good helps too. Even though I don't know how I'll find a way back, Quinn insists there's a way. Just that it will take time to find. That I can't rush it."

She frowned a little. He'd mentioned this person before. "And who is Quinn?"

"A consciousness embodied in the castle now. Separate from the castle's typical magic." He shrugged as he leaned against the counter. "The castle—and by that, I mean the building—broke apart during the battle. It was scattered as well. Enough of the functioning magic imbued into it keeps it running, floating, and mostly hidden. But I don't have enough magic to guide it or to make it move in accordance with my will at all. Volsrei cursed us to never touch the land before our final battle. He cursed us many times, and that one stuck. In one of the other conflicts, all at once, this consciousness was imbued into the castle itself."

"And that consciousness calls themselves Quinn?" She blinked. The assorted spices she had gathered blended easily. Carefully, she rubbed them into the duck. "Did Volsrei create them? Who is he, anyway?"

From the way Traelan had reacted and the way Ryul had spoken, it was obvious they agreed on how horrible he was.

"A necromancer and warrior who attempted a bond with my kind and others and who tried to take our skills for his own. Among other things." He picked up the onion and peeled it. "My family and a few others opposed him publicly, and it got worse from there. But whatever consciousness was imbued into the castle, we don't know who they are exactly. They won't say either except that they will protect us. They spoke more to my siblings than to me initially. When the castle itself shattered, I don't know if their consciousness fractured out into all those pieces or if they just stuck with me. Quinn themselves does seem like they're slower and angrier lately. Far more protective than they used to be."

"Well, if someone tore me apart and sent my consciousness in lots of directions, I probably would be upset as well." She put the duck into the pan and then popped it into the oven. These were odd types of magic, but she vaguely recalled hearing stories of such things.

"Fair enough. They don't let me into the armory or

a lot of other places, and it's often a battle of wills, though it is getting better. They just say they don't want anything to happen to me."

"It's surprising they let you do anything with your magic then."

"Probably because that room has no walls. That and the old ballroom just rotate out there. What remains of the castle is really more of a ruins. At the end of every lunar, it seems to fall apart more and more. One day—" He scoffed, shaking his head. "It's still beautiful, though. The ballroom is my favorite place to go. Whenever I need to think, I always go there. Especially when the sun is setting and the moon is rising."

"You just watch the sun set?" It had been a while since she had taken the time for that, but she could envision him doing that so easily.

"If I have a big decision to make, yes. Though lately, as soon as the sun goes down, I am on my way here. I want to be here almost more than anywhere."

Heat rose through her chest and spread into her face as if she was crouched in front of the oven. "Sometimes, it's nice not to be alone," she said softly.

It wasn't just because she was afraid something might happen to Ryul. She actually liked his being here. His presence soothed and warmed her all at once.

"Quinn has told me that I must at least consider that this is where I must remain. This realm might be the one I have to remain in. They told me that back when we nearly crashed at the edge of the wilds and the cavern. And it has been many lunars now that I have tried to become enough. I was angry. And frightened. I can't accept that I won't find them. I don't accept that. And that has made it hard to heal. Since I have met you, though, I don't struggle as much with the thought that I must remain here for a time. I used to think that accepting this meant I was giving up on what I wanted. But it isn't. That's—I'm not saying any of this well. But it's because of you. You've made my life better."

"You've made my life better too." She ducked her head.

"I'm grateful for your friendship, Erryn," he said.

"I'm grateful for yours." Her heart clenched tighter. She bit the inside of her lip. "Would you like to talk about your family?"

He nodded as he continued to slice the onion. "It would be nice to talk about them if it wouldn't bore you."

Nothing he said could bore her, really.

"I'd love to hear about them."

He shared about his family as well as their journeys to find their parents and aunts and uncles. It wasn't just a small group of them either. A whole host. Well over a dozen names. Possibly more. Siblings and cousins, all banding together. Each one had magic that tended toward a certain affinity. Particular forms and strengths that they focused on.

"Mine was supposed to be the fire-breathing garm," he said. He scratched Buttons' ear. "But ever since the fight with Volsrei, well—cute as Buttons is—he's the best I've managed. He was the first time I even managed to get a coherent shape. Everything else was just smoke globs that evaporated."

"Do you think perhaps your magic has just changed?"

He laughed mirthlessly, his expression pained. "Maybe. And if it has..." Sighing, he raked his hand through his hair. "Well, if it has, it has. And I will probably never see them again."

She shook her head. Her heart clenched. "It wasn't your fault. You've done nothing wrong, and so I'm sure you will. You deserve to find them, Ryul, and I'm sure they are looking for you."

"I don't know how much deserving has to do with this. You could be the best person in the world and lose everyone through no fault of your own." Scoffing softer this time, he worked his jaw. "And I don't think any of us really are without fault. There had to have been something I could have done differently."

Her chest tightened. She stole up beside him and slipped her arms around him once more. He hugged her back at once.

"I'm sorry. I know you miss your family," she whispered.

Though she wanted to tell him that everything would be all right, she couldn't. Because she didn't know that it would. No matter how much she wanted it to be, it might not. And he was right. It wasn't about deserving or what was right in his case.

He rested his cheek against the top of her head. "Deep down, I don't know if I'll ever see them again. And I don't actually know how to fix anything. I just keep guessing."

"You don't have to do it all now," she whispered.

"You just get through tonight, all right? Each day. Each night. You take it as it comes, not all at once."

He hugged her a little closer. His presence warmed her as well. It felt so good to be held this way. He smelled like cedar, solid and comforting.

"Are you all right?" he asked softly.

She shook her head as she pulled free, heat flaring through her cheeks. "Yes. Just have to take my own advice. One day, one night, one minute at a time. That's all." Sniffing, she stepped back and hurried to the counter.

"What about your family?" he asked.

She shook her head firmly, blinking back more tears. "No. They aren't here. That's my fault. And I don't want to talk about it further. Why don't you tell me more about something you'd like to talk about? Maybe about the castle or Quinn themselves if you'd prefer."

"I can do that," he said.

A WARNING

The fear of Ryul's late arrival combined with the terror of Traelan's ambush should have left her raw and exhausted. Especially after sleeping so little and working such long hours. The long conversation about Ryul's home and family as well as the suppression of her own story certainly hadn't helped.

But Erryn found it hard to be still or calm. Her thoughts twisted and turned even as she slept. She woke in a cold sweat. Something had to be done.

Her heart broke for Ryul. By this point, she had pored through every page of the books. Asked everyone she could think of and offered up gallons of soup to anyone who could give her new information. But there were no answers.

People still came for the soup, though. It was a typical day, cooler than before with a crispness in the air. Lanna even dropped off six butternut squashes and over a dozen of the late zucchinis.

Since the days were shortening, autumn's arrival

meant that most of her customers would come between noon and mid-afternoon. Except for travelers who were in dire need. But there weren't that many of them. Especially not this year. In fact, there had been none in dire need. No attacks or threats at all for weeks.

The heat of the mid-afternoon sun was more pleasant today than it had been in a long time. She kept the door open still, the war of the hot fragrant steam and the crisp cool wind making for a delightful contrast.

"I came to make my apologies once more."

She stiffened, her fingers tightening around the wooden spoon. "You really have a lot of nerve showing up here again, Traelan."

Traelan stood in the door, his hat in his hands this time but that mildly cocky smile still on his face. "I do, but that's largely because I have no shame. It isn't conducive to someone in my line of work. That doesn't mean I am unaware when I have done wrong. I invaded your home and threatened your guest, and for that, I am deeply sorry."

"You made your apology last night."

She refrained from offering him soup. The sooner he left the better, though it did surprise her that he was here. There was a genuineness in his eyes at the moment that she hadn't expected. As if he had something he needed to tell her.

He twisted the hat in his hands. "I am leaving this afternoon."

"I hope you find what you are looking for and do

not invade anyone else's home in the process," she said coolly.

He chuckled, his tone surprisingly good humored. "I understand your anger with me. Ryul seems a gentle soul. Particularly for a blood fae. But I came here to caution you even more. Especially as I interrupted what looked to be a tender moment."

"He would not hurt me, and..." She stopped before she reiterated her stance of not making bargains or deals with fae. The first part was enough.

He nodded slowly. "No, I don't believe he would willingly, but he is very young."

"Maybe for a fae," she laughed. "Two hundred seventy-eight is hardly—"

"Months. Not years."

"What?" She blinked, trying to run through the numbers. "So he's—"

"About twenty-four."

"I—I'm older than he is?"

She'd never even met a fae who was less than a hundred years of age. This felt wrong. And strange! No wonder she'd beaten him so easily. It no longer felt like such a triumph.

Traelan nodded. "I'm not telling you what to do. I wouldn't dream of such a thing. Especially when it comes to matters of the heart. But as you're alone here and you don't have any family of your own, I'll tell you what I would want someone to tell my own sister or cousin. Young fae fall in love hard and fast, especially if it's their first time. He doesn't even know his own heart or his own mind in this. And the feelings alone aren't enough to determine what is truly within the heart or what will happen over the years."

"We all change with time," she said softly.

She wasn't who she used to be. Not at all. In both good ways and bad. Yet pangs of unease twisted through her. Why did this even matter? It wasn't as if she was going to get into a relationship with him and had to be prepared for all the changes he would go through as he gained his new powers.

Right?

"Yes," Traelan said, "but the changes that he will go through are dramatic in comparison to what humans do. He hasn't even grown into his wings yet. While relationships happen and there are no laws against fae of his age entering into relationships or marriage, most do not. Most families do not permit it or bless it, and as someone who fears open-ended bargains and rejects them, you will need to be exceptionally cautious. Young blood fae feel with their entire beings. But feelings change fast. And that wish that is required? That's part of its purpose. To test the sincerity of the bond beyond feelings. It's not as simple as the blood fae choosing the proper wish in response to the statement."

"Part of its purpose?" She frowned. "Then how is it twisted to cruel ends so often?"

She'd heard many stories over the years of humans who fell for blood fae and spoke those dangerous words only to be sent on impossible quests or ordered to walk off cliffs or cut out their own hearts.

"Who is it protecting?" she asked.

"The wishes will be twisted to reveal the truth of the

fae in mind and heart alike. As I said, feelings can lie. And some blood fae do use it cruelly. Most of the decent ones will warn any they meet against developing such feelings."

"He did warn me."

It had seemed insulting at the time, but the warning was real.

Traelan nodded as if he had guessed as much. "Yes, and already he is wavering. I can tell you that just by the way that he looks at you. Even though he does have other desires that are prevalent. To find his family again. To restore his magic. Whatever the blood fae wants will rise to the surface when that wish is offered. What will you do if one of those desires slips out in his wish? If the truth that lies within his heart is that he cares for you but not more than his family and power? The irony in this is that it is the cruel who wind up with the most power in these wishes because they have so little feeling for the one who makes it that they can focus on what would be most advantageous and use it to their advantage. Ryul is young and untested, and he will likely be swept away. To your great misfortune. It is not at all likely he will have the skill or the strength to chain his own heart in response to the power of that wish, and that is why that truth will be revealed and why it is considered unwise for anyone to make such a bond. The temptation is powerful. Despite blood fae being permitted to wed after twenty-one years, most avoid it until much later for that reason, among others."

She remained silent, biting the inside of her lip.

"I know this may sound cruel, and I know that you

may think you have the solution. He will as well, almost assuredly. Why must you say the words? Hmmm?" He tapped his finger to his temple. "Such a good plan. Such a simple one. Don't say the words. Don't offer the wish. Don't create the conflict. But as soon as the feelings start to grow within you, more and more will happen to compel you to say them. It's part of the process. I have known many through the years. None have resisted the pull. Those words, simple as they are, cannot be held back once they are felt. Not forever. Best to kill the feelings early and fast or end the connection entirely. Best not to even think them or say them at any point. As you are older than he, you will have to be the strong one. Unless you fancy destruction. You can consider this warning to be payment in light of my earlier offenses."

"Given that you barged into my home, threatened my guest, and now have come to give me unrequested advice, perhaps you could do one thing for me that would actually help."

He chuckled as he placed his hat back on his head. His loose brown curls shifted with the movement. "Given the nature of the advice I have provided, one might consider the debt paid."

"One might, but I do not. How can I restore his magic?"

If she could restore his magic, then she could send him on his way. That was the simplest way to complete this. Fulfill her promise to him, and then…

Her entire being ached at the thought of never seeing him again, but was there any other way?

Traelan clicked his teeth. "You yourself can do nothing. Nothing in this world that can restore it beyond its own natural rate of replenishment. Were we in another realm, that answer might be different. Were he a different kind of fae, that would also be different, but he is a blood fae. A very young one from a family that separated from the traditional path and as a result is even less typical in their physiology."

"There has to be something!" She struck her hand against the counter. "You of all people, who travel throughout this world and presumably into others, who gathers up ancient artifacts and runes! You have to know something. What is it?"

Chuckling, he set his arms akimbo. "Would you make a bargain to restore his magic or gain such knowledge?"

"Is that what it requires?" She scowled at him, but everything in her tightened with fear.

"That's not the question I asked."

Her stomach sank. She clenched her fists. "If a bargain was available, that means that there are ways to negotiate. I would find a way to make it work without a bargain. There would be a trade. A clear and manageable trade."

He smiled. "Well, fortunately for you, there are no bargains to be made, or else I am afraid you'd find yourself in far over your pretty little head. But that just isn't how blood fae magic works. Especially not his family's."

"So you know his family?"

"I know of them and of the sacrifices they made. If what Ryul says is true."

"He wouldn't lie."

His brow quirked upward. "You know this for certain, do you?" He smiled. "Not that I doubt him either. But as we were discussing earlier, things can be incorrect without being lies. Mistakes happen. And more importantly, there could be unintended consequences. Volsrei was a dangerous man with skills beyond most of his kind, yours, or mine."

"And what kind are you, exactly?" she asked.

His smirk returned. "I'm not in the mood to divulge that. I hope that everything comes together for you, though. You two do seem quite sweet together."

"We aren't a couple," she said tightly.

He shrugged. "I suppose we shall see. The one bit of comfort I would give you if you want to help him is this: good food and kind company are among the most healing elements in all the worlds. You've likely done him great good already. I hope that time is gentle with you both. Until we meet again, Erryn."

DEVELOPMENTS

Traelan's words left her with a lot to think about. The nature of the wish that had to be granted when a person told a blood fae "I love you" unnerved her all the more now.

If someone wanted to examine her heart fully and completely for the truth of what she believed beyond the emotions, how would she stack up?

How would anyone?

Weren't they all complicated individuals?

That truth didn't make it any safer, especially when she hadn't told him everything.

Ryul's arrival that night did not settle her mind any further. Perhaps it was the fatigue catching up with her.

At his request and because the night gryphons weren't out, he took Buttons out to play again. She peered out from time to time, touched by how sweet he was with the little dog.

The mushroom leek soup had nearly finished

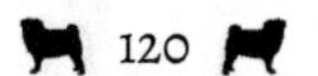

cooking when she looked out once more. Ryul had unfurled his wings and was crouched beside the dog.

Had there ever been anything sweeter?

She covered her mouth, her heart swelling with warmth and happiness.

His wings had spread broad and full, the top portions slightly more visible, especially along the frame. Faint hues of lavender and blue caught in their lines. One wing did not seem to catch the air quite so well, and depending on the angle, large sections of the lower wings went invisible.

As he coaxed Buttons, he remained on the grass. He flexed his shoulders and wings, hopped, and thrust the wings down to show the movements.

Like Ryul, Buttons struggled to catch the air or do more than flutter for a beat or so. Each time he landed, he yipped and then jumped at Ryul's face. All the while, he wagged his tail. Sometimes, that almost seemed to help. If he ever did fly, it was probably going to be more like a bumblebee than a dragon.

Another perfect moment. She shook her head. Was this how all blood fae trained their flying beasts? Somehow, she doubted it, though this did seem more natural than when he had been attempting to teach Buttons without his wings unfurled. That made her heart warm all the more.

The moon had well reached its zenith by the time the soup was finished, and Buttons eagerly lapped up the water she had set out for him. Ryul likewise drained half a pitcher of water.

"I can't say I was expecting you to give him such

intense flying lessons tonight. He seems to be making good progress," she said.

Ryul wiped his mouth with the back of his hand. "He's a long way from knowing much about it. More importantly, we're going to have to work with him if he's going to be even a halfway decent watch dog. When that person barged in last night, Buttons didn't do anything except try to hide."

"Well, with a name like Buttons, what do you expect?"

"He can learn, and he should protect you. Maybe he can't track and fight, but he can learn to protect at least a little."

She dished the soup into the bowls, hoping he wouldn't see her smile. The thin slices of mushroom bobbed in the creamy broth. "He protects me from loneliness. That's all he needs to do."

"He can do better than that." He took the bowls from her, his hand grazing hers before he placed the bowls on the table.

Her heart thudded faster. She swallowed hard as she pulled down two of the mugs, tucked them in her arm, and picked up the pitcher. At least once they were eating, she'd have something to do with her mouth.

He groused further about Buttons needing to train and learn. Sometimes, though, his gaze fixed on her, soft and warm, his words slowing. Her insides twisted. Using words became more challenging.

She didn't fall in love easily. Not anymore. At least, that was what she had wanted to believe, but regardless of her intent, she was slipping.

Buttons didn't seem aware that he was the subject of the conversation. He came to lay between their feet as they ate the mushroom leek soup.

"It's just going to take time," Ryul said, "but that would seem to be the one thing we actually do have."

She nodded in agreement, her insides still fluttering. Buttons would learn to be a strong guard dog and a watch dog if Ryul had anything to do with it.

Cleanup took even less time than usual. He helped her wash and dry dishes, prepared some of the onions and celery for tomorrow's soup, and swept. Then, before he left, he pulled her into a hug with both arms.

"Have a good night, Erryn." His lips brushed her ear before he pulled away.

She barely suppressed the shiver that spiraled through her. "You too, Ryul," she said, steadying her voice. She scooped Buttons up and held him close to give her something to hold. "We'll see you tomorrow."

He nodded and crossed over the threshold. She followed him to the edge and watched as he strode out into the night. He was halfway to the tree when he turned. Her heart leaped into her throat.

"It won't be night again soon enough," he said.

"No one can stop the night," she responded. She pressed her chin to Buttons' head, holding the little dog tighter.

His grin became a crooked slash of white. His purple eyes sparkled. "I'll be here as soon as the night returns."

Oh, Creator save her.

Traelan was right. Ryul had fallen for her because

he didn't know the truth about her. This had to be stopped, even if she didn't it want to. This could go nowhere good.

The following day, she handled her usual tasks and considered what she could do to convince Ryul that he deserved better. Much, much better.

For once, she might have been glad to see Traelan, but true to his word, he had gone on his way.

Night no sooner came when Ryul was at her door again.

"You should take Buttons out to play," she said, stumbling over her words. "He's been unusually active. I haven't seen hardly any night predators out lately for a while now, so you know we might as well take advantage of it because you know they'll be back with a vengeance."

Buttons barked, though it sounded more questioning. As if he wondered what he had been doing that would make her say such a thing.

"And give him more flying lessons," she added.

Ryul tilted his head. "Are you all right?"

"Wonderful. Just excited to see this little dog learn how to be all he can be."

He grinned then. "He'll be flying in no time."

"Good," she said. "That's what I want to hear."

She then thrust Buttons into his arms and hurried back to the counter where she resumed slicing radishes and potatoes with surgical precision.

If she told him about what had happened to her—what she had done to her own family—that she had lied to him—he would certainly want nothing to do with her then. It would mean also the loss of his friendship. And that...that broke her heart just as much. But it would be safer for both of them.

There wasn't a way to stop these feelings from developing and still be around each other.

The thought of going back to the long lonely nights pained her. Even her music wouldn't comfort her then.

No. There had to be another way.

So she stalled.

Ryul cooperated, though sometimes his hands brushed over hers, or he stood a little closer than usual. More often than not—when she caught him looking at her in that soft warm way, she wanted to collapse against him. Each night, when he hugged her before he left, she wanted to curl deeper into his arms and bury her face in his chest. Sometimes, she had to dig her fingers into her palms to keep from thrusting them into his hair and leaning up to kiss him. And each night, it got harder and harder to step back from his embrace. The thought of telling him anything that might make him dislike her grew harder as well.

For a time, it worked. Occasionally, he protested her sending him out with Buttons despite there being no predators about, suggesting instead that he remain in and help her, but he always complied after she asked whether Buttons was in good fighting condition yet.

One night, the storms came again. He came in drenched, rivulets of water running from his hair down his chiseled cheeks and jaw, his doublet clinging to his hardened body.

"Your creek is turning into a river," he announced.

She darted into her bedroom. "You're soaked! Are you all right?"

Part of her had hoped he wouldn't come that night, and the other part was glad he had. She pulled the large coarse towel out of the closet and turned. He'd followed her in.

Oh.

Stiffening, she hugged the towel close.

He glanced around the small room lit only by the candlelight from the main room. Then he gestured toward the lute resting in the corner by the wall. "I didn't know you played."

Her throat thickened. Forcing a smile, she stepped closer. "Not often and not well. Here." She offered him the towel.

He held out his hand, his gaze raking over her.

How was it that he wasn't even touching her and her body felt like it was on fire?

"Here." She tossed the towel over his head so she didn't have to see his achingly handsome face and darted past him. "I need to start chopping."

Hurrying back to the counter, she pulled out the ingredients. What was she even making tonight? Lavender potato soup with crumbles? That no longer seemed like such a good idea, but she couldn't think of anything else. Lavender supposedly had restorative properties, but it wasn't the easiest ingredient to incorporate into soup.

She grabbed up the onions, potatoes, lavender, and spices and set them on the counter. There was just enough cream in the icebox to be sufficient.

Her heart was still fluttering and battering about when Ryul returned. His pale-lavender hair had mostly dried and fluffed, and he patted at his chest and shoulders with the towel. Then he set the towel aside and pulled off his doublet.

Well, polph.

She looked away, then glanced up. The pale-blue undertunic clung to his ridged muscles and emphasized his cut shoulders and collarbone.

Pressing her lips in a tight line, she resumed organizing her spices. Was he doing this on purpose? He might be. Why did he have to be handsome, charming, and thoughtful? If he was only one of those things, it would have been fine, but somehow, he was almost everything.

As she finished organizing her spices and ingredients, he picked the towel up and draped it around his neck. "What can I do to help?"

Somehow, his offers to help were stirring her desires even more than his good looks. Somehow, she had to do what was best for both of them and not let the feelings develop any further.

"Um, you could separate the lavender buds for the soup. Do you know how to do that?"

"Yes. Did someone find this, or did you purchase it from the town? I've heard it's expensive in many of the human places, and you can't harvest it from the sky."

"You harvest it from the sky?" She laughed, the tension coiling tighter within her. "I've never heard of that. No. Here it just depends. It isn't so bad in these parts, really. Besides, I never really splurge on things.

The last time I did was on a dress. Which was a big mistake."

"Why?" He tilted his head, his brow drawn up in a questioning expression. "Even if the dress was not a beautiful one, it would be so on you."

She pursed her lips. Damn him for making this so much harder than it had to be. How was she not supposed to fall in love with someone like this? Maybe that was part of her punishment.

"It was a mistake because I have nowhere to wear something like that. It was just extravagance. That's all. And I should have been smarter than that. Women like me don't need fancy dresses."

"Maybe what you need is a reason to wear one. Maybe it's enough just if you want to wear it. Unless you were waiting for someone special to make the moment special."

She hadn't told him about that little dream. Had he just guessed, or was she simply that easy to read?

She cut off the end of the onion, trying to think of some way to change the subject. Some way to start pushing him away.

"So." She peeled the onion carefully, letting the thin yellow-orange skins fall into the small pile. "I heard that you are actually very young."

"Two hundred seventy-eight lunars," he said. "Old enough to fight and fly and almost as tall as I'll ever be."

"You're more than tall enough."

"How old are you?" He gave her a coy look.

"Old enough to do whatever I want." She tried to

give him a playful smile as she started chopping the onions.

It was easier to see now how young he was. Though he didn't seem to be acting nearly so innocent. Perhaps he had fallen in love before? Her gut tightened. Barely twenty-four. No wonder he'd been so easy to beat. His powers would go through so many changes over the upcoming years. There wasn't such a huge gap in years between them, but she wasn't going to go through some sort of metamorphosis in the next decade.

She cleared her throat. "And none of your business. Besides, it's irrelevant."

"I don't really understand human aging anyway. Isn't it all rather moot?" He moved with surprising precision over the lavender, separating out the buds and the stems. "The differences in lifespans can be addressed."

"If we have access to the healing fountains and restorative pools, yes. But the years aren't the point. We humans grow up fast. At least compared to your kind." She chopped the onions slower. "Sometimes, maybe we should grow up a little faster. We also stop getting new abilities and such that would transform us like your kind."

"It seems to me that humans go fast enough as it is, and I am old enough to do whatever I want too. Except —" He shrugged. "Well, it doesn't matter. Unless human women prefer fae to be significantly older than they? Does my age bother you?"

"For what?" She raised an eyebrow at him. "I'm

making you soup to replenish your magic to buy a dog. You're old enough to make trades. That's all that matters."

"What if I wanted more?" he asked, cutting his gaze to hers. He pulled another of the spires of lavender out of the bundle.

"More soup?"

"No. And Buttons is yours. I wouldn't take him from you. Wouldn't turn him into anything either. I like him. And..." He pushed a fresh lavender spire over her hand. "Maybe I might like you. I know most fae who pursue humans are significantly older and far more experienced. I am neither. But I want to share those years and learn with you."

Heat flared through her, but she kept her gaze on the cutting board and the sweet onion. He had to let this go. They both did.

Except—she didn't want to.

He tapped her with the lavender as he leaned over the counter, staring at her intently. "What about you?"

"I like Buttons too."

She scooped up the onions and dropped them into the pot rather than sweating them first in the skillet. Polph. It didn't matter. It didn't! She hadn't even remembered to put the skillet out.

"I think you might like him more than you like me."

She laughed weakly as she moved back to the counter.

"Do you like me?" he asked, softer this time.

"Yes," she said, still refusing to look at him. "You are very sweet."

He brushed her cheek with the lavender spire, tickling her sensitive skin. "You're sweeter."

It was hard not to smile. If he had any sense about him, he wouldn't be paying any attention to her.

"Have you ever been in love before, Erryn?"

"Hm?" She blinked, freezing in place. "Um. Yes. Well, more crushes than love, I suppose." Mostly unrequited. "For real, once or twice."

Her heart clenched hard as more bad memories pressed against her. She thrust them back. Her hands shook.

"What were they like?"

"They who?"

Her cheeks burned. She struggled to even look at him, but she could practically see those warm amethyst eyes studying her even when she closed hers. Could practically feel his arms around her again.

Traelan was right. Those words were bubbling up inside her already.

"Whoever you fell in love with."

"You don't like me like that, Ryul." The words were little more than a whisper.

"Who are you to say?" He spoke lower now, firmer. As if he guessed what she was doing and had decided to stop her. "Who are you to say what I feel? Is it because I am not yet a century in years? You don't think I can know my heart? That's not right, Erryn. All you can say is what you feel, and I say what I feel."

She kept her voice firm as she picked up another onion. "I'm a soup maker who works out of a cottage I don't own on the edge of the Barrens Wild. What kind of a future do you really think I have?"

"What kind of future do you want?"

She pressed her lips into a tight line. Why did he have to make this so difficult? What did she want? A future with him. Yes! How ridiculous was that!

He placed the lavender spire on her hand. "I think you could have any future you wanted."

She brushed it aside. "No. Not everything is possible."

"If it was possible? Assume it is. Whatever it is."

She swallowed the words, then set down the knife. Her hands were shaking far too much. Her mind blanked on what to say next. She massaged her fingers.

The silence intensified between them. The fire crackled and popped, and the bone broth in the second pot bubbled and hissed against the lid. It was going to cook down too far if she didn't finish chopping the rest of the ingredients soon.

"I don't know if this helps," he said slowly, "but I was thinking about when we talked the other night. When you said that nothing would happen between us, you didn't talk about your feelings. You said it was about the bargain and that you weren't any good for me. Now, I disagree with you passionately on the latter, but for the former, I just—I don't need you to ever say that you love me, Erryn. And if you never say it, you never get involved in the bargain."

She shook her head. No. No. She should have stopped it sooner. Should have found some way to stop all of this.

"My point is..." He brushed the tips of his fingers along her arm and hand. "I do love you."

"Ryul, you shouldn't."

"Why?" He shook his head, his expression bewildered as he circled around the counter. "Why shouldn't I? Even if you killed someone—"

"You deserve better than me. All right? When I was a girl, I was very selfish, and I did about the worst thing I could to my family outside of directly selling or murdering them. Let's leave it at that."

He frowned. "What? I thought you didn't remember. I don't understand." He shook his head. "But I don't have to. You don't have to tell me about anything you don't want to, unless you're planning on killing me. Or something like that. Whatever happened when you were a girl, well, you're not a girl anymore. No matter what you have done—"

"It would not be wise for you to trust me. Hasn't anyone told you that humans are capricious and dangerous?"

"All sentients are, and all make mistakes. I don't care what you've done, Erryn. You don't have to tell me about your past. You don't have to talk about it at all. We all have our secrets, and I'm not judging you on who you were. I am judging you based on what I have seen and know of you. Of all these things. That you were willing to risk your life for Buttons."

She scoffed. "I don't think that's—"

"Nothing is really guaranteed, is it, Erryn?" He caught hold of her and pulled her near. "But I am willing to take a chance on you. I will bet my life on you."

She closed her eyes but did not move away. Her breaths dragged free, shallow and ragged.

He stroked a knuckle from her temple to her chin. "Does clinging to this provide any chance for the past you abhor to be fixed?"

"Nothing can be done to fix it."

"Then don't stay with it. Come with me. Let's make the future better." He nuzzled her, lingering against her cheek. "Just because you made a mistake doesn't mean you have to stay with it forever. I know it's dangerous to fall in love with a blood fae, but I swear to you that this I know: I won't hurt you. Ever. And I accept you. I don't need you to be someone else. I just need you to be you, and that you includes who you were before."

She leaned against him, savoring the warmth. His lips brushed her cheek and then trailed to the corner of her mouth. She stilled, holding her breath.

Was he going to—

His lips brushed hers then.

Her heart pounded faster, her eyes fluttering shut as she melted into the kiss.

It wasn't her first kiss. Not in any sense. But none had swept her away like this.

He savored her, his lips soft and gentle as he slipped one hand up her back. Then his tongue pressed to her lips, nudging them open. She moaned softly into his mouth. That was it.

He seized her, arms wrapping tight around her and pulling her hard against him. His hands gripped her hips, his fingers digging in just enough to make her gasp as he deepened the kiss even more.

Her hands traveled along his powerful chest, feeling the hard muscles beneath his thin sleeveless tunic. His heat radiated into her, intensifying the passion that coursed through her veins. She moaned again. Her entire body had come alive at his touch. Her head spun. She was drowning in his arms, and she never wanted to break free.

Except—polph!

She thrust her hands against his chest and leaned back. "Wait." She gasped. Her hands shaking, she pulled free. She had to get this out before she lost her nerve. "You don't understand."

"Don't understand what?" He steadied himself, blinking. "You want to stop? We can stop," he said reluctantly, his hand sliding to her arm. "This is—what do you need? Just tell me. Whatever you need —anything."

She held her hands up. Part of her wanted to just disappear back into his arms, to hide in his embrace and disappear into those kisses and more. But it wasn't right.

"I need to tell you something. I lied to you before. I do know what happened! I betrayed my family. They are gone because of me!"

She pulled back, her voice tight with tears. A few trickled down her cheeks as she tried to choke them back. In all the years since it had happened, she'd stuffed the story deep inside her.

He tilted his head, his brow furrowed.

The way he looked at her now—he wouldn't look at her like that any longer once he knew the truth. That was why she had to tell him. This had to end. There was no way around it.

A BAD BARGAIN

Erryn ducked her head, bringing one hand up to her eyes as if she could block his gaze. The words pushed out slowly, as if they now had a mind of their own or as if some magic had summoned her confession. There was no way to stop them, no matter how much they hurt. How horrid that it was here, with the one person whose respect and good opinion she did not want to lose.

"My mama tried to raise my sister and me well," she said hoarsely. "Always reminded us how blessed we were to live in the northern islands. Humans don't fare so well in some places, but here—or rather there? Peaceful. Good laws. Plenty of food, even if you were poor. Plenty of places to shelter. Eventually, I hated it. I wanted something better. Sometimes when we fought, Mama said I was ungrateful, and I was. After all, when my dad died, we didn't lose our home. The people in our town helped when it was needed. My mama was able to take in work doing various odd jobs. We even got a bit of an education. It was a quiet but good life.

"Both my sister and I reached a point where we were to choose what employment we wanted. Mama wanted us to take on full trades to take advantage of the opportunities available in our town, but I thought I was meant for something much better. A singer and a dancer. And I would travel over all the world and be the most beautiful, the most melodious, the most best of all." She attempted a small flourish, then hugged herself. Her chest tightened as she stepped back again. That sick pit in her stomach expanded. "I wasn't going to be a weaver or a fish chopper or a servant or someone who did odd jobs. Especially wasn't going to work at the tavern, even if it was a good one where we wouldn't be at the whims of customers or reliant on tips. I was going to find my calling as a singer.

"It seemed for a while like that was the clear path, no matter what Mama said. After all, she and my sister encouraged me to sing and play. They said it was my gift. And I wanted that to be my true career. If this was my gift, why shouldn't I make it my life? Except there were no opportunities for singers and musicians in that place. All I needed was time and the opportunity, but none came, and I didn't have enough money to leave. My mama didn't want me to leave either. Most other places were dangerous, she said. Especially for a young woman all on her own.

"My sister started working at the tavern. It was hard work though good, but it made her plainer. Wore her down. I said I would rather die than work in such a place. She didn't write any of her poems any longer. She didn't draw or paint. When I asked her about it, she said it was just for a time. A season."

She swallowed hard, pressing one hand to her face. It was like living it all again. Shame flooded her. She didn't dare to lift her gaze to his. How could he not judge her?

"Before that, I'd been coming around to the realization I'd have to give up my dreams. But…when she said that—something snapped inside me. Mama told me I had to choose a place to work. I had until my sixteenth birthday. I thought it was grossly unfair. So we fought. And fought."

Her heart beat faster. The memories grated through her mind, sharp and painful. Harsh words echoed within her mind, painful as the day she had spoken them. She dug her fingers into her skin.

"The fighting got bad. I said terrible things to her. To my sister as well when she tried to stop the fight. And then I said I was going to go to the Cabin. It was this little place up on the cliff where some of the youth would go to be alone. I was going to stay there and forage until I found enough to pay my way to one of the cities. She told me that was good. I should go and stay there. Take care of myself. See what it was like to not have a family. All I had to do—all I had to do was put the glow markers on a white boulder at the crag's edge. You could see the markers even from our house, and she would know that I was safe. Simple, right?"

More tears sprang to her eyes. She scrubbed them away. Regret choked her.

"My first night there, I set it up. Set up the boulder. Put the markers on it with my sign, and I did what I usually did. It wasn't the first time I'd been up there to think, but it was the longest. Days turned into weeks. I used up everything I had. My foraging and bracelet weaving wasn't enough to gather enough coin for more than a few nights of travel if I didn't want to sleep out under the trees. Ultimately, there was nothing. Not even a surprise friend or a bolt of inspiration. Even after the food ran out, I tried to stay in case there was a miracle. But two nights of that, and I just—I realized I needed to go home and accept the truth, so I started back, and that's when I met her." She paused, trying to catch her breath.

He poured her a glass of water and set it beside her, but then he stepped back so that the gap was not closed between them. He watched her with quietly contemplative eyes, one arm resting on the counter.

The fire crackled, sparks popping as the wood shifted in the grate.

She couldn't even take the glass of water.

"I met a night fae," she continued, her voice thick. The words came, slow and painful. "She saw at once how talented and beautiful I was. Or so she said. And she had a special gift for me. Well, not a gift as it turned out. A very special bargain for a very special girl. She would let me go on a grand and wonderful adventure where I would be revered and adored. In the cities. At the festivals. I could make my name and my fortune, and everything would be honey and roses for my family and me. All I had to give her was a day and a night of her choice." She closed her eyes and pressed her hands to her face. "It sounded so wonderful, you know? Just a day and a night. That was all. Not the day or night of my birth or of my death. Just an ordinary night and day. For some reason, I assumed that it would be the next day and night. That I would go through, experience it, and when I came back, it would just be a day and a night while I had all this fortune and all this good to share. What was one more day and night? Mama might worry if I missed one night, but it wouldn't be so bad. Besides, I'd find the solution. Maybe she wouldn't even notice? I thought I could get in in enough time that she wouldn't—"

She covered her mouth. It had been stupid. Tears brimmed in her eyes.

"I took the bargain. Let her make the mark. At first, it was so big. It covered my neck and shoulder. Over time, it has shrunk down so most can't even see a trace. She hadn't mentioned that, but I didn't mind. This new adventure was wonderful. People were throwing themselves at my feet. Everyone raved about my talent and my skills. My voice. My presence. My poise. Everything. I performed better than I had in any of my dreams. Until I realized—it wasn't real. There were holes. It was—it was nothing but glamour and falseness. I pushed through the illusion. I made myself real, and I tested myself. Only to find...I wasn't even average. Once I saw through the falseness and the glamour and realized what I really was, I pushed through the rest and found myself back in that clearing. It sickened me. I couldn't even carry on the pretense or hide in the illusion. It was over."

She covered her mouth. The memories hammered at her harder now. It had been so much worse than she could put into words. The jeers, the screeches, the yells. The utter disdain once the glamour no longer masked the fae mark. They'd realized she was a fraud, imbued with magic to perpetuate what they deemed to be a scam. Some even seemed to know about her family. They yelled so loudly and accused her of murdering her mother and sister with her carelessness. It was as if they had seen straight into her heart and taken every fear and turned it into verbal daggers, hurled at her with vicious accuracy and thunderous volume that even now had her cringing. All so loud it had beaten into her ears. Even now, there were times when simply voices that were too loud sent her back into that place.

She ducked her head, trying to rush past those memories. If she told him everything that happened then, he might feel like she was trying to make him feel sorry for her. That wasn't what this was about. Her breaths became tighter.

"I got home." Barely. "Ashamed and exhausted. When I got back, though, someone else was in the house. Everyone—everyone was shocked to see me." She hugged herself tighter, shaking her head. "Time didn't stop while I was gone, Ryul, and it wasn't a random night and day the fae took. She took the day I left for the Cabin and the night I put up the boulder with the markers. So Mama didn't know where I had gone. She didn't know I was safe all that time. She and my sister went off to look for me. And—there was nothing for them to find."

"I'm sorry," he whispered.

She dared to glance up. He wasn't looking at her. His focus had turned toward the fire now, and his brow furrowed. It was starting. The contempt. The rejection.

It was all right, though.

This was what had to happen.

It was what she deserved.

Just as she had deserved it when they had driven her out of that town.

"I don't expect you to agree with me." She struggled to steady her voice. "Or to even feel sorry for me. I sacrificed my family in that bargain, and I lost everything. I am a horrible person. I was old enough to know better. And it really doesn't matter that I didn't intend those consequences. They are what they are. My mama warned me against making bargains of any sort. Especially ones involving glamour and magic. But I thought I knew better than her. Now she and my sister are gone. The terrible thing I had to realize is that... there was no way that played out without them suffering in some way. What I did was selfish and cruel. When I realized what had happened, I ran away. I was terrified. Then I started searching for them. But it did no good. They are lost. Probably dead because of me."

"Do you know that for certain?" He continued to gaze at the fire, his expression inscrutable.

"I've looked everywhere I can. Even tried to make a few more deals. But I didn't have anything anyone wanted. Then—" She wiped her hand under her eyes.

"Well, after a certain point, it became obvious. Especially after what the crowd said. I think somehow they knew. The magic revealed it. And some of what people said—I don't think they made it."

"May I ask? Why lie about not remembering? Why not just refuse to tell everyone?"

"It was easier. Everyone could see the mark the night fae left on my shoulder anyway." She fussed at her sleeve. "Even if they can't see it, a lot seemed to guess. Something about the way I carry myself, I suppose, and memory loss is a common side effect. No one really pried beyond that. Especially since Nan found me halfway up that staircase in the forest."

"You mentioned that earlier," he said, tensing. For the first time, he looked back at her. Anger or fear flashed in his eyes. "So you weren't coming out of the portal. You were going into it. Erryn, don't you know—"

"I know what they are. Or at least what they seem to do. But it didn't seem important at the time." She hesitated as she met his gaze.

That was the part he wanted to focus on? A fear that she might cast herself to death and the unknown through one of those doorways? She deserved far worse.

"But that isn't what matters. What matters is that I shouldn't have made that bargain to begin with. I gave them up for literally nothing."

"Erryn—"

She held up her hands, shaking her head. The tears couldn't be stopped now. "And truth be told, I should not have made the trade with you for Buttons. It was dangerous, and I'm fortunate that you weren't someone who would twist my words against me."

He moved beside her. "Well, the words of your trade were well chosen." His hand brushed over her arm. "As were your knots."

The tears built within her. Why was he trying to make her laugh? She covered her mouth.

"And this situation—this bargain you made with the night fae—this is what you think makes you a horrible person? The reason that no one could or should love you?"

She nodded tightly.

"Then, please let me address your points again. So far as you not being worthy of love, Erryn, I disagree. And your mother and sister would as well. Mistakes were made. Regrets formed. But that was years ago. How many I can't actually say since you won't tell me how old you are."

"Old enough to know I can't make it right." She pressed her hands to her eyes.

"Probably not, but it doesn't mean you should punish yourself for the rest of your life. It doesn't make the situation better. It doesn't use the life or the skills you have."

"How can you even look at me?"

"How can I look at you?" He tilted her chin up. "You're the most beautiful woman I have ever seen. Not just physically either." He leaned in closer, his breath caressing her cheek. "You're brave, strong, clever, and compassionate. Yes, you made a mistake, though I certainly put a lot of blame on the one who offered you that bargain to begin with, but if you could fix it you would. You're imperfect but still deserving of love and happiness. How could I not look at you? I don't want to look away."

Her heart skipped a beat as she stared into his eyes. Of all the things she'd expected him to say, this wasn't it. How could he be this wonderful? How could—

She closed the space between them and thrust her lips to his.

Groaning, he swept his arms around her and crushed her close. His hands roamed her body, pushing her into him as she thrust her fingers through his silky hair.

He ignited a fire within her that she had never felt before. She twined herself closer, holding him tight. Those three words burned inside her. She wanted to say them—needed to say them—and then they'd both be tested.

A cold bolt of realization struck her. She pulled free, panting. "Wait. I'm sorry. Ryul, we're going too fast. We have to be smart about this."

"Smart?" He gasped. He stepped back, wincing. "How so?"

"I haven't given you any time to process what I've told you. You may feel differently about me—about us once you do. And then—what I want to say—what I will need to say—if this doesn't stop, what happens next?"

He laced his fingers together and rested them on top of his head. "All right." He closed his eyes for a moment, then shook his head. "This is fast. And that wish will test us. It will tempt me. We should be ready for it." He released a long slow breath. "So I'll think long and hard about how I feel about a woman who made a bad bargain when she was a child. And you think about whether your past should bind you and whether you can accept that someone actually wants you. Let's take seven days to think about this then."

"Yes." She nodded.

The deep desire that swelled and burned within her continued, but those curls of unease helped her restrain herself. She pressed her fingers tight against her palms. She wanted him, and he wanted her. That wasn't a guarantee it would last. The thought of offering an open-ended wish also sent her into a near panic spiral each time she considered it.

"One week. That's good."

"Good. And, in recognition of how much you hate to lose or be wrong, I dare you not to fall in love with me more before the end of the week. And I double dare you not to say it." He flashed her a coy smile, his manner seeming to ease. "All risks aside, I'd never let you live it down."

"No, I doubt you would."

She bit the inside of her lip. It was hard to believe he hadn't turned on her. All this time she had held this in, and she had never considered that someone would accept her once they knew it.

Fear tightened throughout her body. What if he changed his mind? But what if he didn't? And then what would there be?

"I suppose this means we should refrain from kissing until all this gets settled," he said reluctantly.

"If we want to be wise about this, yes." It hurt to say those words. "Not that I don't want to—"

He shook his head, whistling low. "I know. Probably shouldn't talk about it, though, because it's taking all my strength to not just swoop you up and—" He released another breath, a low near-growl following. "I am not actually sure what to do with myself now."

"I know." She wiped her hands under her eyes again. Her chest remained tight, but it was easier to breathe. "What about helping me make the rest of the soup for tonight?"

"That works," he said with that soft smile. He removed one of the knives from the wooden block and cut off the ends of two parsnips. "I'll do whatever it takes to make you happy, Erryn."

TIME AND FAMILY

It was a strange thing to have suddenly told the truth of what had happened to her family and yet not face the condemnation she had expected. Erryn wasn't sure how she felt about it entirely, and the shock combined with her desire to be with him pushed down some of the grief.

They passed the rest of the night talking, though. This time about her life. What she had done. How she had traveled. How she wound up here at the edge of the Barrens Wild. Not a particularly interesting story from her perspective. No battles or quests or wondrous deeds like his family had.

But he listened as if it was the most fascinating thing he had ever heard. Whenever she reached a topic she didn't want to talk about and voiced that, he apologized and redirected. The way that he listened and responded warmed her even more now.

Despite the teasing tone of his dare, it was true. She was going to lose because she already felt that way. The fact that he let her have her space and didn't insist on kissing her or touching her or trying to coax her into giving in early only heightened her desire for him.

He arrived each night. What he thought about when they were apart, he did not say. But he took Buttons out to train him and helped her with whatever she needed. He spoke easily about all manner of things when the conversations grew heavy, and he didn't disturb the silence when she needed to remain still.

Perhaps he was right. Each day that she contemplated the matter, the more she had to recognize that her mother and sister had both only wanted what was best for her. Giving up her dream enough to survive was necessary in this world. They had seen her limitations, loved her, and wanted her to be able to find her own way. Even her sister had not said that she would never take up poetry or drawing again. Only that for a time, she was too weary.

That was life.

There had been many days when Erryn herself had felt so tired from her work and travels that she had not been able to think. Her work here in the soup cottage wasn't so difficult or challenging in the summer and early autumn. But winter through early spring, it became far more intense and required almost all of her energy and strength because the travelers who did come through were often needier, the regular customers almost always far hungrier than usual, and sometimes more dangerous individuals walked these paths. Winter's chill brought many hungry mouths.

Seasons came and went with different demands.

Their change brought about distinct expectations and experiences. You couldn't hold on to the heat and slowness of summer when winter howled outside. And if you tried to maintain the rapid pace of the winter soup cottage during summer, you'd run yourself ragged and for no reason.

Did that mean that there was a season in which to say goodbye to old wounds and errors?

But even if there was, could she step headlong into another open-ended bargain with a fae who couldn't even guarantee his control of the wish to be asked?

There was no way to make what had happened to her mother and sister right, and she couldn't think about them without her heart sinking and her stomach clenching. If she dwelled on them too long, she started hearing those booming voices jeering and condemning her, mocking her for the stupidity of her choice and blaming her for all that had happened.

But somehow—in the quiet moments of chopping vegetables or the louder ones of running with Buttons or the peaceful ones just being with Ryul in the darkest hours of the night—somehow, a little space formed in her heart. Space to recognize her own future and to ask herself what she wanted her life to become rather than insisting she drift along.

There would be other ways for her to honor her mother's and sister's memories. Perhaps something more productive. It grew easier to contemplate.

What remained, though, was the disturbing reality that if she chose to be with Ryul, there would come a time when she would say that she loved him. Traelan was right. Already, the words burned inside her, especially as clarity refined the feelings.

The thought of making such an open bargain—especially when he might not be able to fully control his response—sickened her. Not because she did not have feelings for him. Creator help her, her heart thudded faster every time his image reached her mind or his name rose in her thoughts. No, if anything, her feelings strengthened by the minute.

Taking this lesson from her mama and sister and then turning around and granting an open wish in bargain to a blood fae felt—wrong. Somehow. Questions rose within her, each one demanding attention and trying to shake the foundation of who he was and the wisdom of their being together. No matter how she tried to move it around or reframe their situation, their being together romantically was not wise.

But her heart didn't care.

The sincerity in his eyes, the tenderness in his voice, the calmness in his manner, all of it made her heart flutter. And no matter what soup she made, even an ill-advised honeysuckle black bean and a poorly constructed green soup, he ate it happily.

There had to be a way to make all this come together.

On the seventh day, a wagon pulled up outside the soup cottage late in the afternoon. The familiar jangle and rattle of the harnesses and shuffling footsteps sounded like Nan.

That was odd. Both late in the day and early in the month for her to be visiting.

Wiping her hands on the towel, Erryn went to the weathered wooden door as Nan approached. The old woman moved with a heavier stride than usual, her black triangular shawl wrapped tight about her shoulders despite the warmth of the golden autumn sunlight. Her dark-blue eyes were watery and red-rimmed.

"Nan?" Erryn pressed the door open farther. "Is everything all right? Do you want some tea? The water isn't hot, but I can put it on."

"No, no need, dearie. I can't stay long." She entered the cottage, moving with an uneven shuffle. She looked far older than she had the last time they had spoken, and the merriment wasn't present at all.

"What's going on?" Erryn hugged herself, her own unease intensifying.

Nan finally looked at her. Pronounced bags darkened the skin beneath her eyes as if she hadn't been sleeping. She tried to smile, but it faltered. "I'm so sorry. This isn't how I wanted it to be."

"Wanted what to be?" She stopped herself then, stiffening. Oh. "Ina's coming back? You need me to leave." A dull ache formed within her chest.

"It's not just Ina." Nan bit her tongue, then shook her head as she closed her eyes. "I don't know what's happened to my girls. But all of them—they've all taken leave of their senses. And they can't stay in the city any longer. So they're all coming home. All of them. And all at once. Not one or two at a time. I have to find some place to put them all. And my own house is nearly full with Marcus there with his knee done in and Teino after the fire. Auntie Plum needs more care than ever now."

"I see." Erryn hugged herself tighter as she cast a glance around the cottage.

"I thought it was just going to be Ina. But it's Ina, Seren, Lysa, Vira, Oriana, Rosa, Claudette, and Micha. All of them and the little ones. And Marcus can scarcely even walk." She dabbed at her eyes with a handkerchief. "Poor choices were made, dearie. Very poor choices. They tried to hide it much as they could. Then Seren and Ina and Lysa tried to run. That just made it worse. Should have told us the truth from the beginning. They should have, but they didn't. And I am sorry. I am so sorry to do this to you. You don't have to leave if you can tolerate all these changes. You can stay through winter, but there'll be another six people staying here come tomorrow morning. I know that's not fair to you. That it's hard to live with one or two new people afoot, let alone five and a newborn. Maybe two more little ones as well."

Her stomach sank still further. There certainly wasn't room in here for all that. At least not easily.

Nan kept her head down. "I couldn't turn them out on the streets. It's just gone from bad to worse. Can't see how much worse can happen, short of death. Not that I'm asking for that, but I'm not turning you out either. My word to you stays. I'll bring in blankets and pillows and all the rest. We'll make it work, if you're willing. But I also won't force you to stay either. I don't think I'd be capable of staying with so many underfoot, but you're not me. Whatever you want to do, I will respect it. If you want to stay here for a day or three or a week or all the way to the start of spring, I won't refuse. If you want to leave at once, I won't refuse you that either. I'll put in a good word for you at the Broken Cauldron if you'd like to work there."

She nodded numbly. "And the soup business?"

"You don't worry about that, dearie. You think about what's best for you. The weather is good now for travel if you wanted to try for somewhere else. And if you need a wagon to take you someplace, we'll find a way for that. I'm just—I'm so sorry."

"No. It's fine. It was only for a season anyway," she said softly.

Maybe it was a sign. Everything changed. Even this. In the past, she'd talked so much about wanting to go out again and wander and go on adventures. Now that she faced it, she wanted to roll back the day and start over, skipping this part. But there was nothing to be done except accept it.

"Don't worry about me. I'm going to be all right." She forced a smile. "What do you need done to the cottage for their arrival?"

"If you can budge up your stuff so it won't take up as much space and they'll have room for their things, that'd help. But really, there's not much. Just take care of yourself and try not to think too harshly of us."

A whistle sounded from the cart.

Nan covered her eyes. "I'm sorry I don't have more time than this. There's just so much to do." She started toward the door. Tears glistened in her eyes and down her cheeks as she turned her face away.

Erryn followed, slower.

Loto sat in the wagon, his left leg heavily bandaged with colorful strips of cloth. He sat hunched with the reins loose in his hands, his heavy slate-blue coat bunched up. When he saw her, he gave a weary nod, his steely-grey eyes also duller now. "Sorry to do this to you, Erryn," he said. "We'll try to give you as much space as we can."

"I'll be fine. Neither of you worry about me." She gave her arm to Nan as Loto helped Nan up the rest of the way. "I'm sorry for whatever has happened."

Best not to ask for details. No one needed to know all that. She wouldn't want her grandmother telling everyone about her mistakes.

"Bad things happen." Nan situated her dark-burgundy skirts around herself as she sat in the coach box. "We all make mistakes. I'm glad they're coming home. We'll find some way to make it work."

"All we can do," Loto said. He adjusted his weathered brown hat and then sighed. "Take care now, Erryn. At least you'll get to meet the girls soon. Try not to judge them too harshly. Rough days for them lately and all."

He clicked his tongue as he moved the reins, and the grey mule started forward with an easy step.

No. She wasn't going to judge anyone harshly.

Forcing herself to smile, she waved at the old couple as they left. Whatever mess their grandchildren had gotten themselves into, all those two wanted was for their little family to be happy and healthy. Touching and tragic all at once.

The heaviness intensified as she watched them disappear down the path and toward the town. Despite the offer to let her remain, that wouldn't work. Not with Buttons and Ryul. There'd be too many questions. Too much drama. Too many problems. She'd have to find somewhere else.

She glanced up at the sky. Only a few hours more until dark. She covered her mouth. As if she and Ryul didn't already have enough to talk about.

PRISM

Erryn peeked out through the windows at the almost-full moon. He was late tonight. Was everything all right?

The stars glistened in the sky, bright as illuminated diamonds in a bed of midnight-blue velvet. Even now, the air smelled of the rich autumn meadow flowers in their final days as well as woodsmoke and the hay harvested from the fields to the south and west. The cool breeze fluttered the curtains.

An anticipatory heaviness hung over Erryn. She had already chopped all the onions, carrots, celery, parsnips, and other vegetables for the soup, even though she hadn't fully decided what type it should be. Vegetable something, clearly.

What had happened?

The door clicked open.

Her heart leaped.

Buttons trotted to the door, barking, his ears pricked forward.

Ryul stepped through. He glanced to her, his face lighting up at once. That big smile on his face warmed her through. Then he bent and pet Buttons. "Didn't realize it would take me so long to get here tonight," he said.

"As long as you're all right."

She hugged herself. Her stomach was all aflutter. For now, his being safe was really all that mattered, wasn't it? Everything else was up in the air. Where was she going to go from here? Could she trust him with the wish? She couldn't answer those questions. But she wanted him to be all right. To be happy and safe. Even though she couldn't really believe that his happiness would involve remaining with her.

"I want you to be all right."

His smile went crooked, making her stomach flip again. "I'm more than all right." Straightening, he stepped inside and closed the door. "But there is something I need to say. Something I realized and that I've wanted to say all week, and I just ask that you hear me out."

She braced herself. Of course he'd reached that conclusion. Whatever he had to say, it was going to hurt. If he was smart, he was going to tell her that they could not be together. It wasn't wise. Nothing against her. Just—someone like him with so much ahead of him and so much change could not risk being tied down to someone like her who was—static.

Yes. Even if what she had done was forgivable—even if that could be set aside—they were entirely separate beings from entirely different backgrounds. Even if she did say those words and allowed him to request any wish, his truest desires, when spoken, would not reflect her. And that would just put her at more risk. Really, for both of their sakes, this was best.

She could practically hear him saying the words, and tears misted in her eyes as she prepared. It had to be this way. She was going to go back to being alone and wandering, but at least this way, she wasn't going to wound anyone else.

He fidgeted, shifting his weight and scratching the back of his head before he looked into her eyes and squared his shoulders. "Like we agreed, I have been thinking a great deal about our situation, and I have come to a conclusion. I know that this wish business is terrifying. That for anyone who is intelligent, it should be addressed with extreme caution. After what happened to you with fae bargains, I cannot blame you for being uneasy. So I have been conducting my own research. Quinn isn't pleased with me, but that hasn't kept me from finding what I think is a solution."

"A solution?" Her brow tweaked. That wasn't what she had expected.

He placed a small grey box on the counter. Stepping back, he folded his arms. "It would take quite a lot of self-control to never say certain words that you feel. I don't need to hear you say them. Your actions—the way you look at me—all of that is more than enough. And right now, it probably would be dangerous for you to say them. You'd have to trust me in a way that is far too much to ask right now. So this is for you. It isn't a bargain or a trade. It's just a gift that might prove useful."

Frowning, she lifted the lid. Inside lay a rose-gold necklace with a heavy prism. "It's beautiful."

Even in this low light, it sparkled, sending gold and pale-pink fractures of light across the room. What was it for, though?

He placed a small pot of ink and a narrow quill on the counter. "It's something someone in my family found a long time ago. They stuck it in a box with some notes. Apparently, it binds words or phrases. You write the phrase out on the prism in this ink. And as long as you wear it, you can't say that phrase. It can be a little uncomfortable to wear if you really want to say those words. But as far as Quinn and I can tell, it's just a suppressive. It doesn't draw power from you beyond the initial words, and you can take it off in between if you would rather not wear it."

If he had brought this, then...

She picked the box up and studied it. "So you still want to be with me? After everything—even if I can never say what I feel exactly?"

His smile softened. "The only other thing I have wanted more is to have my family back. And you don't have to use this or keep it. Because you're right. I could be jumping ahead. I don't know what you've decided. You may have concluded that it is far too dangerous to be involved with someone like me. And if that's what you decide, that's all right. I love you. I love you, and I accept you as you are."

His words sliced into her like a blade, piercing

through her and pinning her in place. The way he said those words—his voice firm but heavy with emotion. She felt them within her as if he spoke them straight into her heart.

"Over the years, you and I will both change," he continued. "It is what living does to everyone. There is no guarantee aside from our words and our vows to one another to be faithful. And those can, of course, be broken. But, for what it is worth, I mean these words with every fiber of my soul and every breath in my being. Yes, I am a blood fae, and yes, I have several changes ahead of me and much to learn and many new ways in which to grow. What won't change is the fact that I love you. I have been working on what wish I would make to honor our love and bind us if you should ever decide that you can trust me enough to make that wish. But even if you can never say it, please know that I love you. That I will always love you."

Her cheeks and neck burned. She brushed her fingertips over the prism, her other hand cradling the box. Could it be this simple? Could something that seemed too good to be true actually be true?

"We're both lonely," she whispered hoarsely. "Cold beds and empty arms could push you to make a bad choice for your future. You may find after you are less lonely that you will change your mind."

It wasn't hard to imagine that he would have been quite lively at parties and would have quite the social life if his magic ever returned and he was able to go back to his home. The way he had kissed her both those times had been pure ecstasy. It wouldn't be long before he found someone else.

"I was lonely. But not since I met you. I would take a cold bed and empty arms for much longer if it meant eventually you would be the one in my arms and bed."

She hugged the box close, her fingers curled over the corners.

"Don't you want to be with me, Erryn? Answer that question. Please."

Her lips trembled. Was it possible? Could she really be with him without having to enter into some magical open-ended bargain?

"What is your family going to say if they find out that while they were gone you got married to a human woman?"

"We'll just be so happy to see one another again, I doubt they'll think to criticize anything except the way I've cut my hair or what I've allowed Quinn to do or how I've managed the magic of the castle. Besides...I've been looking for them since I was two hundred and five. I won't ever give up looking for them, but Quinn is right about that. Even if they are surly with me right now. I can't put my life on hold until I find my family again. There is no way to make my magic come back together faster. And this time I have spent with you is the best of my life. So is that your only objection?"

"I have absolutely no magic, and you are magical," she said. "What about all the opportunities you're going to miss in your life by being with someone who isn't magical?"

"Your smile is magical." Ryul tilted his head down, trying to catch her gaze. He moved closer.

She pressed her lips together, fighting to restrain the smile that was springing up. "Ryul."

This was foolishness.

"I feel magical when I am near you."

"That's not magic. That's—" She covered her face.

"I know what it is, but that doesn't make it feel any less magical. Doesn't even mean it isn't magical, actually."

She fought both the smile and the tears that wanted to rise. "Stop saying that things are magical. Especially me."

He caught her hand in his and brought it to his lips. "There are all kinds of magic out there. I'm offended on your behalf that you can't see just what makes you so magical."

Her heart fluttered as his lips touched the back of her hand. How much better would it be to kiss him as well? All these feelings—all this inside her beyond the fear—perhaps it *was* magical in its own way.

"I don't know if I can be what you need me to be. I don't want to hold you back."

He drew her closer then, one arm hooking around her waist. "All I need you to be is you." His lips parted as he leaned closer. "Erryn, you are more than enough for me just as you are."

Her breath caught in her throat. She wanted to seize him. To close those few inches between them and seal this bond between them—no matter the cost. To feel even more of his hardened body against hers—to drop back into that heated passion from the week before.

And those words rose within her.

Those three words.

She ducked her head, then picked up the prism. "How do I use this?"

If she wasn't careful, she was going to burst out and say it.

He smiled then, making her heart swell with such emotion she thought it might burst. "You need to write the words you bind from your mouth directly on it."

She placed the prism on the countertop and picked up the quill. The cap from the ink pot opened with a satisfying sound and released the strong sweetly metallic scent. As she dipped it in, she prepared herself.

It was simple. All she had to do was write those three words, and she wouldn't say them.

But it didn't feel right.

He had offered this, and it was generous. There was no treachery in his eyes. No harshness or hidden deceit. She'd heard of similar forms of magic. As far as that went, it was one of the safer kinds. But something about this felt wrong.

She hesitated. "If it is this simple, why do others not do it?"

He shrugged, his brow tweaking. "What do you mean?"

"This seems like a simple solution. Like putting extra potatoes into a broth when it's too salty. It's so easy...and either it's rare and it was just lying around and you found it, or it is something else." She tapped her finger against the prism. "I think it's something else, isn't it?"

His brow furrowed. "It will protect you. You won't be bound to me or anyone."

"What is the cost of this magic, Ryul? The real cost? Traelan told me that those words will be almost compelled from me the more I feel for you. That there is no way around it. That eventually, I will have to say it. He never mentioned that any blood fae might see it even as an option. From what you and he have both said, it sounds as if it is a requirement. And if it is a requirement and it is not satisfied, that means someone is paying. And usually quite a lot."

He shuffled his feet, avoiding looking into her eyes. "It's a price worth paying."

"What's the price?"

She picked up the prism and turned it over in her hand. There were strands of something woven into the chain and sealed within it. Scrawled along the bottom in fine print was the statement, "I pass all costs of these bound words to the one whose hair is enclosed in this prism."

She held up the prism. "Is this your hair in it?"

"Possibly."

"Explain this to me."

He shrugged, then sighed, his shoulders dropping. "It's a transference prism. I don't know all the consequences that will come from using this to hold back those words, but this way, they won't harm you."

"And you think that would be acceptable? I don't want you to get hurt either."

"I can't imagine I would get hurt."

"It's a magical prism that transfers consequences! How could it not hurt you?"

"Well..." He looked up at the ceiling. "I don't know how to make this safe otherwise."

"It isn't safe!" She set the prism aside and set her hands on her waist. She almost started laughing then. "Ryul, I won't let you be risked like that."

"How else can I kiss you then? How else can I show you everything I want to show you?"

She ducked her chin, then rubbed her forehead. "There's something else too. And I probably should have told you sooner, but I thought you were going to tell me that we needed to part ways."

"What have I done or said that would make you think I would want to be away from you?" He raised an eyebrow.

"You said that I needed to hear you out. That usually means whatever follows is going to be bad."

"Oh...I just thought you were going to argue with me about using the prism. Which you did. Just not for the reasons I thought."

She gave him a small but sad smile. "Protecting me shouldn't get you hurt. Though the thought—that means everything to me."

"And you shouldn't have to give me a wish. Just being with you is enough for me."

"It's not how life works, though, and we shouldn't do something stupid just because we don't like something in life. Believe me, I know. I'm older than you."

He wrinkled his nose at her. "You can't be that much

older."

She folded her arms. "But the other thing is that I will need to leave. Nan needs this place for her granddaughters. She said I can stay until I get on my feet, but it's going to get crowded here, and I don't know how Buttons will do. Or how they will respond to you. So I won't be here tomorrow night."

His eyes widened, all traces of amusement fleeing. "Where will you go?"

"I'm not sure yet. Probably just wander again. But I'll find some place where I can make you enough soup to finish paying—"

"No." He shook his head then stopped. "You can come stay with me."

"Stay with you?" She blinked. "How would that work? I barely know you. Won't Quinn object—"

"I don't care." He stepped closer, taking her hands in his once more. "It will just be us. If Quinn has an issue, I will address it."

This was not a solution she had considered. But maybe—maybe it could work?

"Besides." He tilted his head slightly and flashed her a mischievous smile, the corners of his mouth turning up slightly as he spoke in a soft yet playful tone. "You just said you owe me soup. It would be much easier for you to fulfill the terms of our bargain in the castle rather than me having to chase you around the edges of the Barrens Wild or wherever else you'd take it in your head to go."

She stared up into his beautiful amethyst eyes, then nodded slowly. "All right. Let's go."

FLEE

Moving into the castle with Ryul didn't resolve the problem of the wish, nor would being in close proximity with him result in anything aside from an intensification of those feelings. But suddenly, it felt like the most sensible thing in the world to do.

Buttons yipped and scampered about, excitement shaking his body. It was as if he had realized all was well now, and he made up for all his previous silence.

She really didn't have much at all. A few items of clothing for different seasons that fit handily into her old rucksack that she'd first come here with. A couple additional odds and ends as well as her lute.

"One day, perhaps, you'll play it for me. I'd love to hear your songs."

"Maybe."

She hadn't ever played for anyone to hear her except Buttons after she realized the truth of her skills thanks to the night fae, but she was glad to be taking it with her.

She filled the one rucksack and then one other smaller woven bag. In this one, she placed that beautiful purple-pink gown she'd bought on impulse as well as her hairbrush and her last handkerchiefs. The bag was so light it felt like nothing over her shoulder.

One last thing was to write a note to Nan, explaining her decision. Nan would likely be disappointed, but in the end, it was better this way. And nothing said she couldn't return to visit some other time.

Ryul picked up the rucksack and slung it over his shoulder as she protested. "I can help at least a little," he said, "and if someone needs to carry Buttons, he'll prefer you."

"Fair enough."

As they stepped through the door into the coolness of the night, she took one more look over the soup cottage. For so many years, it had been her home. A temporary place that had become something so much more long term. If she ever found some fortune of her own, she hoped to return and repay Nan and Loto's kindness. She hoped also that things would go better for them as well, even as all their granddaughters returned and all the challenges that would bring.

Tears stung her eyes. Saying goodbye to the soup cottage was like saying goodbye to an old friend. The weathered wood with its charmed and warded trim and the grey stones that formed the rough path had faded even faster over the course of the past summer and autumn. Bits of moss and mushrooms grew on the north side, and the roof sagged a little to the east. But all these years, it had stood secure, chimney always streaming a low line of woodsmoke and the air permeated with all the delicious scents of soup and home.

Ryul waited for her a pace or two ahead, his expression contemplative and his hand on the rucksack.

"I'm sorry—" she started.

"There's no need for apologies. It's a good little cottage. If it had a consciousness, I think it would be similar to yours."

"If it had a consciousness, it would probably have quite a lot of stories to share."

She turned her gaze up into the darkness of the night. What time was it? The hours were passing fast, but surely they could still make it.

"I'm assuming we cross the boundary marker, but after that, I'm not so sure."

He extended his hand to her, his eyes bright with emotion. As she placed her hand in his, he drew her closer, his touch warm and reassuring, sending a shiver of delight down her spine.

"I'll show you the way."

With that, they made their way toward the boundary marker. Then, together, they stepped beyond it. A sense of adventure and anticipation filled the air as they ventured forward.

She walked over the scrub, her boots crunching lightly over the dry grass. Ahead lay the great wall of tall trees with high boughs that blotted out the sky and seemed to slice the Barrens Wild in half. Over the years, she'd made a few brief excursions out that way but never far.

The air smelled damp and thick with earthy scents as she stepped into the forbidden forest space. The change in the air struck her at once, almost suffocating in comparison to the open air beyond the boundary marker. Every time she had dared to come out here, it had always struck her how much harder it was to breathe. How much more unnerving.

Even if she hadn't seen much to terrify her in this place, she knew it existed here. Not evil, perhaps, but cruel, hungry, and unfriendly.

Yet Ryul guided her forward, his manner calm and unafraid. Why would he be? How many times had he traveled through this place to come see her? It had been nightly now for weeks. Had he ever been afraid of it?

The darkness deepened, and the path grew more difficult. With every step, Ryul seemed to know exactly where he was going—picking out faint trails in the undergrowth and taking them deeper and deeper into the old forest. After a few minutes, she picked up Buttons so that they didn't risk losing him.

"How dangerous is it out here really?" she asked.

"How do you mean?" He guided her a little to the left, and a branch scraped over the side of her head.

She glanced up into the sky again, even though she couldn't see it through the thick branches. "This time last year and even up through the spring, there was just so much more life and danger in the skies. You couldn't walk out here hardly at all. But for weeks now, I've scarcely seen any monsters at all. It's as if there aren't any predators about at night. Is that just out near the boundary markers, or is it true of this place as well?"

"There's been a lot of strangeness. I haven't seen the predators either," he said. "Sometimes the wind tastes faintly of magic, but I've never been able to place it. There haven't been as many monsters, but there has been more travel through these parts. The footpaths to the west and north are all more worn down than they were even a week ago. Do you not get many travelers through these parts? I don't know whether it's more or less for you than usual."

"It hasn't seemed like there are more travelers recently." She frowned. Traelan had arrived a relatively short time after that started. Perhaps that was part of what brought him here? He'd been talking with Povro who specialized in protection charms and wards.

She continued. "We get travelers in all seasons, but these parts have never been heavily populated. And never so many that it disrupted the creatures. What's odd is that there just haven't been many creatures about."

"Well, I wouldn't say that this area is heavily populated," he said. "And I haven't actually spoken with any of these people. I only see them from a distance. Watch your head. Come a little closer to me now. There's a boulder there."

She could vaguely make it out, but it didn't bother her that he was walking her through the path. "I suppose your nights have been rather occupied."

"Perhaps a little." It sounded as if he was smiling.

"What do you think is leading to the gryphons and such being gone then? Any thoughts?"

"It seems to me they just might have moved on. It hasn't tasted or smelled like anything that would destroy them, and I haven't smelled blood. It would be hard to kill them without creating at least something of an odor."

"I suppose so. Not that I miss being terrified to go out at night. Buttons has certainly enjoyed getting the extra exercise."

"He'll have lots of fun roaming through the castle. Even with it only being a fragment of what it once was, there's plenty of room to explore. It's part of the reason I don't like being there when it's just me. It's too big." He halted, then moved his arm around her waist. "This log may be a little tricky."

As he pulled her snug against his muscular body, her heart fluttered faster.

Tricky was one way to put it.

She let herself nuzzle against him and breathe in his cedary scent, her feet scraping over the log as he lifted her up and over. As he set her down, she got her footing once more.

"What happens to you if you are out when the sun rises? You can't touch the ground, but can you be out of the castle and just not on the ground?"

"Oh. No. With my magic as it is, I can't be away from the castle for long. The curse will evaporate me and pull me back down into some deep dark place. I can't get out right before the day ends most of the time."

"Does that hurt?"

It sounded awful.

He shrugged. "Sometimes, it's worth it to stay out long enough. When my magic is stronger, I'll be able to fight it. Quinn tries to help me reconstitute or guide me back as the situation requires. But when I'm sent to that place, not even Quinn can reach me through more than words."

"So Quinn isn't in all of the castle?"

"No. Quinn is—well—Quinn does what Quinn wants for the most part. I'm not sure I fully understand it. Before, they could be in a few rooms. They've been trying to deduce some way to end this for almost as long as they have been a part of the building. And being separated from the rest of my family hasn't weakened their resolve. They get upset when they can't figure out how to make it all work."

She frowned as she contemplated this. Sometimes, he had waited until close to dawn to leave for his home. It wasn't something she'd really considered until now.

"Have you gotten…evaporated because you stayed with me too long?"

"If I could do it over, I'd have done it more often."

She could just imagine that soft little smile on his face, but she didn't like that he avoided the question.

"Were you hurt?"

His arm tightened around her waist as she continued to hold Buttons. "The real curse is when it keeps me away from you."

The underbrush started to thin. The sky above

lightened to deep blue streaked with the dark branches. They were nearing a clearing or the end of the forest. Fewer weeds and ivies snaked around her boots. Buttons wriggled with excitement. His barks grew louder, his wings twitching.

Up ahead, she could make out the break in the branches and foliage. It was a clearing. The underbrush crunched beneath her boots.

And then a faint golden glow caught her attention. With each step, it grew stronger. There was more than one out there too.

Torchlights. That was what it was. Several of them. Suspended in the air above.

Her mouth fell open as they stepped out into the clearing. How was that even possible?

Up above floated the ruins of a castle. It was like something out of a dream. Despite its size and weight, it hung effortlessly above the ground as if suspended by invisible wires. The enormous chunks of grey granite blocks looked as if they weighed no more than clouds. Platforms and sections rotated slowly through the air while the central section of the castle remained mostly stationary despite its worn exterior. The once mighty and imposing stone walls were now pitted with holes. Some had cracked and shifted over the centuries, lichens clinging to the sides and moss trailing off in thick tendrils.

She squinted. It looked as if some great force had struck the castle in at least three points and shattered it to bits. Scorch marks scarred broad portions. A few of the windows had been cracked and warped while

doors were missing on one of the towers. Even with all its loss, it was still massive. Dozens of people could live even in this place with ease. How many could have lived in it when the castle wasn't whole?

A set of massive glossy-black doors appeared to be the primary entrance, though the stone walkway leading up to it had been shattered. A half-moon section of a courtyard remained, so close that its rough edges scraped against the outer wall as it slowly rotated with what looked to have once been a ball-room. Half of one wall contained a peeling fresco that was little more than a muddled series of flaking colors.

A chill spiraled up her back. Even with Ryul near her, the cold clasped her tight.

"That's your home?"

No wonder he had wanted to stay away.

He nodded, voice soft but jaw set. "Bit grim, I grant you, especially on the outside. Nothing like what it was, but the rooms I'm in most, I've made comfortable. And wherever you want to be, we'll fix it up. Whether that's with me in my room—or in another room."

The torches provided just enough dim golden light for her to see that curious yet hopeful glance he gave her, and the way his hand grazed her lower back before he slid in closer...A hint of color ran through his cheeks.

Clearly, he hoped she would be in his room.

She turned her gaze up to the castle, her own face hot and her entire being tense. At least this floating castle was a remarkable sight.

She moistened her lips, her heart racing. "It's incredible."

He leaned closer, his breath wisping against her ear. "Wait until you see what's inside."

She shivered. "Well, how do we get up there? It's a little out of my reach for jumping."

"If it were just me, I'd risk flying. But sometimes, one wing randomly gets stronger than the other, and I don't want to crack your head into the stones. So..." He pressed his fingers to his lips and gave a sharp multi-note whistle.

Stones cracked somewhere within the castle, and something heavy rumbled and groaned. Buttons whimpered, pushing into her shoulder.

"The castle itself can't touch the ground, but it can get close. If the magic ever doesn't work, there are climbing ropes as well." He gestured toward an area on the other side of the clearing. "There's a small coil cannon you can use to shoot the rope up onto one of the walls and then climb the rest of the way."

"Climb. It's been a long time since I free-climbed anything."

"Because you're an old lady? Is that what it is?"

She cut her eyes at him. "Remember I know your weakness."

"Yes. I am weak to iron pans to the face," he said wryly. He brushed up against her, his hand circling her hip. "And also to you in general. No ropes required, unless you want them."

She hugged Buttons a little closer, unable to hide her smile.

More heavy thuds resounded above. Then the two large glossy doors lowered. The fractured stones directly before them and around them extended and moved down as if forming an entire passage to allow them entrance. The stones cracked and groaned, bits of rubble sifting off.

That had to be magic. It only smelled like stone and woodsmoke, and even the rocks themselves looked ordinary when still. But there was no other explanation. For not being comfortable around magic, she had gotten herself into a situation where there was more than a fair bit.

Ryul approached the large doors. Though they appeared completely smooth, certain angles of light made images and sigils appear. Perhaps that was magic too? She leaned forward as she tried to make out their meaning. It wasn't so hard to see now. The sky had started to lighten. Dawn was nearly here.

"Hello, Quinn. There's someone I want you to finally meet." Ryul gestured back toward her with an easy wave of his arm. "This is Erryn. She is staying with us now."

Erryn lifted one hand in greeting. Was that the proper way to greet consciousness trapped in a castle?

"Hello."

"No." Quinn's voice boomed out, sounding like a cluster of at least five voices.

Ryul's brows shot up. "Pardon?"

Erryn fell back a step. A branch cracked beneath her foot. That multi-layered voice spoke with such anger. Such hatred. It cut straight into her. The hairs on the back of her neck lifted up as her breaths shallowed.

"She is not welcome in this place," Quinn responded.

Ryul moved between her and the door, setting his arms akimbo as he glared at the doors. His stance broadened. "That is unacceptable. You will not speak to her that way. Besides, this isn't up to you." He rapped on the door, his brow creasing. "Open the door. She is my guest. I say she is welcome here, and so she is."

"Not up to us? My purpose is your welfare. That human is a threat. She does not deserve the shelter of this place. Not after what she has done to you."

She fell back another step. Each word gouged deep within her. Her heart raced faster. The voice was so loud and sounded like so many people speaking all at once. It was hard to breathe.

"That's all been taken care of. It's none of your—"

"She would bind you! She attacked you the first night you met. She beat you. She stole your magic and offered you slop. And she will not take the one step that will prove the bond between you both. She would use that prism to pass all consequence and pain to you. She actively weakens you! She will be the reason for your destruction."

Her head swam. A sour bitter taste filled her mouth. The panicked urge to run filled her. To create space. To escape. Get away. Go! Go now!

"No. I offered it, and she rejected it. And all the rest is settled! This isn't for you to be angry about." Ryul's voice sounded as if it was coming from far away.

She held Buttons closer, her heart racing faster. Each breath was a painful stab through her ribs and lungs.

Ryul crossed his arms. Confusion filled his voice. "This isn't for you to say. We had a misunderstanding—"

"She still does not trust you. She is holding back. We swore to protect you with my life and being. This human bile is not worthy of you. All she has done is wound you and delay you. You could have left by now if not for her! You were willing to bind yourself to endless suffering for her!"

Those words echoed in her mind. Her heart pounded faster. The sound intensified, booming and filling her, multiplying into even more shouts and bellows of accusation. Her stomach lurched. The heavy sounds sent her blood spiking with terror, each syllable cutting deeper and deeper.

Branches prodded her.

It was her fault.

All of it.

Her mother and sister were dead because of her. Ryul would die too. Of course he would. Why wouldn't he?

Quinn continued, "If she truly cared for you, she would speak the words and let you grant the wish, or she would leave and never come back. Her absence is the best she can offer."

Quinn was right.

There was only one thing to do.

She had to run.

Again.

Spinning around, she bolted.

Ryul called out after her, his anguished voice distant and muffled as she sprinted away. She didn't look back, didn't dare to. She had to get away. The castle, the magic, her past, the wish. It was all too much!

Branches slapped against her face, and her feet stumbled on rocks and bumps in the ground, but she pushed through the pain. Tears streamed down her face, and her breaths came in ragged gasps. But she didn't stop until she collapsed onto the ground, chest heaving.

She hugged Buttons to her chest, and he licked at her face, trying to comfort her. But it was no use. She had failed once again. Failed to protect her family, failed to be even close to good for Ryul, and failed to face her own fears.

She staggered to her feet, gasping for breath. The sun had fully risen now, and birds called out, but the world had never felt so empty. Dark gnarled leafless trees surrounded her on all sides.

Buttons whimpered, wriggling in her arms.

"I'm sorry, baby," she whispered, clutching him closer as tears streamed down her cheeks. "I'm sorry. I'm so sorry!"

He licked at her cheek, whining in response.

It had all been ridiculous. A foggy dream with no basis in reality. And Quinn was right. She didn't trust Ryul enough to risk that bond and give him that wish. Why should she be anywhere near him?

She brought disaster and hardship on the people

she loved. That was all there was to it. She'd been a fool to believe even for a moment that there was any possibility for anything else.

Buttons growled, his hackles lifting up. He stared past her shoulder.

"Wh—" She started to turn.

Something cracked her across the back of the head. Sparks exploded in front of her eyes.

She collapsed, Buttons sliding out of her arms. Her eyelids slid shut, his furious barks filling her ears.

Run, Buttons. Run fast.

Then everything went black.

SACRIFICE

A dull pain through the back of her skull woke Erryn. Heat flared against her face as something crackled and popped nearby. A fire, maybe? Wood fire based on the scent.

Cringing, she opened her eyes. She lay on her side, her arms bound in front of her and her ankles tied securely. Whoever had done it knew what they were doing too. There was hardly any give in the thin coarse ropes, but they weren't so taut that they would easily snap or break.

Buttons was nowhere to be seen. Her attacker had put her in a cave, a damp chamber with a single oil lamp fastened crudely to the jagged rock wall. Someone had hewn at this place, leaving pick marks and gouges throughout. Several passages broke off from this room, and a chill emanated from the farthest one.

A small fire burned in the center of the room, the breeze apparent as it drew the smoke out. Perhaps the opening was just on the other side of the bend? That faint yellow light might even be sunlight. Perhaps morning sunlight?

She shifted her weight and strained to look behind her and then to the side, her heart hammering faster. Someone was behind her. A pheasant feather glistened in the low light.

Traelan? She blinked then twisted around to better see. Was it really him?

It was! The once impeccably dressed traveler lay on the ground beside her. Green ropes bound his wrists together and his arms to his sides as well as his legs and ankles. Bruises marred his face and neck, and several charms had been bound tightly to his face. His skin welted and burned beneath those charms. His hat sat on his head at an awkward angle. When he saw her looking in his direction, he managed a wincing smile.

"When I said I'd see you soon, I did not intend it to be under these circumstances."

"What happened to you?" she asked thickly.

“Right place, wrong time. One of my questions answered. Far higher price to pay than I anticipated.” He winced as he shifted his hands. His fingers flexed. Uneven lines ran along them. He glanced back over his shoulder, then lowered his voice. “Listen carefully. Don’t drink anything they give you, and don’t eat anything either. If you cooperate enough, they might not try it, but don’t agree to anything. They’re going to try to make you walk up the staircase and through the doorway in the air.”

She blinked. Her head pounded. This didn't make sense. The staircase? The cursed staircases in the air?

"And whatever they tell you, I don't actually want to eat your soul."

Stiffening, she tried to focus on him. Had he really just said that? Was he joking?

Footsteps scuffed across the stone. A shadow loomed on the wall, and the air chilled. An older man with a braided ash-blond beard entered. His face was weathered and lined, his face and arms heavily freckled with several blue-grey scars curling across his shoulders and biceps amid multiple tattoos of strange symbols, bladed weapons, grey wolves, dark wolverines, and silver eagles. Two swords hung at his side, and a great wolf pelt draped his broad shoulders. He held a dull-tipped spear in one hand. Beads and leather ties looped beneath the head.

"Perhaps this sacrifice will please you and you will cooperate, kytobar."

Kytobar? She froze. That was what Traelan was? She remembered hearing about kytobars a long time ago, but she'd never met one. Nor had she expected to. Or wanted to. They were powerful magic practitioners that ate humans, elves, fae, and the like to gain their powers and maintain their skills among other things, but they never came this far north.

"I don't want another sacrifice," Traelan responded. "All the sacrifices in the world won't change the nature of those staircases and those portals. I'm not helping you. You've disrupted quite enough already, Ilvan."

Ilvan met Traelan's gaze without flinching. "We

have shown you the proper respect, kytobar. If you do not comply, you will force our hand. You can be made to suffer more." His gaze moved to her next. "And, you, make friends with this one. The more he likes you, the more likely this will work and others will not have to die."

"What are you trying to do?" she demanded.

"You will see. Make your peace and become friends. Your time is soon." Ilvan tapped the base of his spear on the ground, then turned and strode away.

She turned her gaze back to Traelan. "What's all this about?"

"They're trying to force open a stable portal at the top of a forest staircase."

"A portal to where?"

"They haven't told me that part. It's not necessary. For now, I am their 'honored guest.'" He scoffed and then dropped his head back against the stone wall. "Good to be honored. Would hate to see what they do with people they really dislike."

"Are you really a kytobar?"

If so, that meant that wasn't his real face. Or his real name. Really, nothing was real about him except his presence and voice.

He tried to smile, but she noticed then how much more reptilian his eyes looked and how his features were almost too symmetrical.

"Like your blood fae's family, I have taken a different path from most of my kind. And I won't harm you. Not that that will keep them from trying to make this work on their own. The fools."

Dozens of questions pressed up in her mind. Some connected, some not. Where Ryul was and whether he was safe. He had to be. But what he must think of her, running off like that.

Her cheeks burned. And Buttons. Poor Buttons.

"Have you seen my dog here?"

His brow tweaked. "That's your next question?"

"I saw him run off," she said. "But I don't know if they caught him."

He paused as if considering this, then shook his head. "To the best of my knowledge, no dogs were brought here."

That was good at least.

She tested the strength of the ropes on her hands. "Do you know what this supposed sacrificial process looks like?"

"Yes. Soon, they're going to take us both out. They'll ask me to share my blood to open the gateway. I'll refuse. There will be some unpleasant threats. That won't work. They'll do their thing. I suggest you look away at that point. Then they'll cut my wrists open and take my blood by force. That will make the portal far weaker than it should be, but it will open a door at the top of the staircase. Then, they will force you to walk through and see whether the portal stays open or collapses or just kills you."

"Oh." She frowned. "I thought those stairways were temporary. How do they know it will be there?"

"They've found a way to hold it in place. But that has its own consequences. They won't stop until it stops them, and that won't be good for anyone. I don't suppose there's any chance anyone would know you're here and in trouble?"

"Not exactly. Ryul might come looking for me but not until after dark."

"Be careful if you try stalling," Traelan said. "Ilvan's temper is short, and Disa sounds friendly, but she gets impatient too. You wouldn't be the first to try to drag this out."

"Who all is here? Can you tell me anything about them that will help?"

Traelan filled her in on what he knew. The camp was made up of five members. Ilvan, the leader. Alrik with the turquoise beads woven in his hair and the silver charms in his beard. Disa, Alrik's sister and Ilvan's cousin, who always wore blue and had a fish hook scar along the back of her hand. Nendri the thin quiet one who kept his beard trimmed and neat but never decorated. And Thurra with the bright-red hair who only spoke when angry or annoyed. They'd caught him two days after he had spoken with Erryn, but he suspected they had been at this since before he had arrived.

"How is it they caught you then?" he asked. "I wouldn't think they'd dare to snatch someone on the right side of the boundary markers."

Heat flared through her, shame tightening in her chest as all the memories of the previous morning flooded back. She shook her head. Poor Ryul. Quinn had been right. She didn't deserve him. She closed her eyes as tears started to run down her cheeks. Would he understand why she'd run?

"Hey, what's this?" Traelan scowled.

"It's nothing," she said, sniffling. "I just—" She shook her head. "I got scared, and I ran again."

"Sometimes, running is the only answer."

"Not when you're running from someone you—"

She stopped. She'd almost said it, and that was dangerous. Biting the inside of her lip, she closed her eyes. If she and Ryul were going to be together, she would have to one day speak those words. Terrifying as it was. But how could she allow anyone the power over her that that wish granted?

"Did he hurt you?" Traelan asked softly.

"Farthest thing from it. I probably hurt him." She explained briefly, trying to keep it focused only on what was relevant. But more than she intended spilled out. Before she knew it, she had told him even what had happened with her family.

Traelan clicked his tongue. "Well, since you know I'm a kytobar, this likely won't be as meaningful. But I've heard far worse. Done far worse. And as far as that voice goes, well, when you're dealing with consciousnesses trapped inside buildings, things get testy fast. Especially if it wants to protect him. What matters, though, is what he thinks of you. And he's smitten. I saw it when I barged in on you. I don't think the feeling is the problem between the two of you, unlike for some. It's that wish."

"Have you ever known a couple who were able to avoid it?"

"No," he said. "Not for long. You can hold it off for a time. But eventually, those words will be spoken. The only way to avoid it is to stay away from him. Which—if things go as badly tonight as I fear, that won't actually be too hard."

No. Ryul was going to come for her. She knew that deep down. Of course he would. She wasn't going to die here. Not as long as she stalled. Among her many random skills, that was one she was quite good at.

She paused then. The way Traelan had said "unlike for some" stood out.

"Did you grant someone the power to make such a wish?"

He laughed softly, but there was a sharp ache in his voice. "What conclusions you leap to."

"Well, you were out hunting blood fae, and you have strong opinions on the subject."

"I have strong opinions on many things, and I am not only hunting blood fae." His jaw tightened. "But—"

Footsteps sounded outside again. The light filtering past the corner of the passage was a dull orange now. Was it time for this ceremony already?

Ilvan returned, this time with Alrik and Thurra. He strode over to her and started to pick her up.

"Wait, wait." She lifted her hands as best she could, the movement small. "I'm not going to give you any trouble. I promise I'll cooperate. The truth is, I'm really fascinated by these portals, and I almost walked through one before but got stopped, so I'm happy to help you sort this out, right? It's not like I could get far even if I tried to run."

"Aye, we'd cut you down before you got more than a few paces." Ilvan scowled down at her, his eyes narrowing and nearly disappearing in the mass of wrinkles.

"Then trust me enough to walk out. I made friends with the kytobar like you said. I don't have anywhere to run, and I am very curious about this staircase."

Traelan nodded, his manner still casual despite his being bound up like a bird for roasting. "It's true. We are friends, and she does like portals and staircases in the forest. She came through one, so I think she might actually have a better chance at surviving this than most."

Ilvan nodded slowly, then stooped and cut the bonds from her limbs. "You keep your word."

"Don't worry. Even if I wanted to, I don't think I could run." She winced and rubbed her wrists, then her ankles. That horrid sensation of pins and needles surged through her, making her shiver. Still she kept her voice chipper, hoping to lull her captors into a more unguarded state. "It'll be so exciting to see where this portal leads. I don't suppose you could cut my friend free as well if he promises not to run away? It would do him great honor."

"No. We don't honor kytobar that way." He took hold of her arm, his grip tight enough it stung. "Now walk."

This time she obeyed, though her legs remained shaky and her hands continued to sting.

Alrik and Thurra carried Traelan out between them, their steps heavy but confident.

Patchy grass and thin firs clung to the rocky soil outside the small cave. An open firepit dominated the center of the camp just a few feet away with two leather tents beyond that before a sheer slate cliff. Large worn leather bags with supplies were neatly stacked beside the tents. It looked as if they had been here awhile.

At the front of the camp though was the staircase, practically glowing in the golden sunlight. Though it wasn't the same as the one she'd climbed to end herself all those years ago, it reminded her of it nonetheless. It was made of round grey stones and had easily over thirty steps and two arches cut in to its broad side. Moss and ivies covered it like a carpet and draped more and more over the sides the higher it went. The one she'd climbed on her own had looked like a giant curling staircase of moss, defying gravity in its steady ascent upward.

It'd take a little bit to climb this. She could get a few minutes stalling in that climb, but that wouldn't be nearly enough.

She glanced around again, searching for something she might use. Large iron stakes had been pounded into the ground at the front and back of the staircase. Though most of the stakes weren't visible, at least from the top, she could see runes had been carved in. Perhaps that was what kept the staircase from disappearing?

At the back of the staircase just beneath the stone platform where the portal would appear, there were two logs situated like chairs on either side of a stone slab with a groove cut in it and a crudely cut stone vessel.

Alrik and Thurra carried Traelan over to it and set him on the farthest log.

Alrik removed a large knife and started to sharpen it. "You aren't going to cooperate this time, are you, kytobar?"

"Can't imagine why I would," Traelan said. "This won't work. And I don't want that one to die either. So, no."

"We have honored you, and we have warned you these past days," Ilvan said, "yet you still respond with such disrespect. Cut him deeper this time."

Traelan hissed in response.

A large black cauldron lay on its side before the cave entrance. Now *that* she might be able to use.

Ilvan tugged her forward. "Start walking up those stairs. This won't take long."

She dug her heels in. "Hey, new friend. I have a thought."

He gripped her arm tighter. "You said—"

"Shh, shh." She put her finger to his lips. "You don't even know what I have to say. Now, my kytobar friend there and I are more than happy to help you get to this place you want to go, but there are easier and better ways. Taking his blood is just inefficient. The whole reason he doesn't want you to do it is because it isn't as effective. Surely you've noticed this?"

Disa and Nendri murmured their agreement low as Alrik gave a loud, "Aye."

Ilvan nodded slowly, his gaze hard. "Go on."

"Well, I don't want to act like I know everything because goodness knows I don't, but now that I see your staircase, I can tell you that the problem isn't with the summoning. It's with the people you're sending through it. If you're going to find a stable path through another realm by taking a magical path, you have to become magical yourselves, for at least a time. And the easiest way to do that is to consume all the components in a simple combination which I prefer to administer through soup."

"Soup?" Ilvan pulled back.

The murmurs of surprise spread throughout.

Disa strode closer, her arms folded over her blue wool gown.

"It must be your real true lucky day because guess what?" Erryn shrugged, then pointed to herself. "I'm the best soup maker there is."

"I think you lie," Ilvan growled, getting in her face.

"I would never lie about soup." She gave him her best and most innocent expression without pulling away. "Blood fae come for my soup all the time to restore their magic. My soup is so good I traded for a magic flying dog. Soup is my passion and my life. If you've been here for any amount of time, you might have seen me in the soup cottage over past the boundary markers right where the forest line and wilderness start."

"Oh, we do know her." Disa strode closer and nudged his arm. "That's the one that sells the chicken barley. Very good soup, dear. Almost as good as home."

"Thank you." Erryn pressed her hands to her heart. "Soup is my art."

"Go on and listen to her," Traelan called. "You all

don't want to be murderers, or else you'd just be killing people to open up these portals. The fact you found me and are using my blood—much as I wish you would not—means you don't want this to be worse than it is. So give her soup a chance."

Ilvan contemplated this. Then he crossed his arms, releasing her arm. Red fingerprints remained on her skin. "Tell us how to make it."

She shook her head and fluttered her fingertips. "Part of the magic is in my hands and the handling of the vegetables and the roots. And it isn't precise. Sometimes it needs a bit more, sometimes a bit less. It's hard to explain."

"I still think you may be lying," Ilvan said. "What're the chances we'd have all the ingredients anyway? There's no way to prove it either way."

"If I am lying, you can always kill me, right? And most of these things can be found."

Ilvan scoffed, his eyes narrowing. "Fine. Build the cooking fire up on the top of the staircase platform. You can prepare it up there. If you're telling the truth, you live, and you can walk through with us. If you're lying, we'll take your friend's blood and push you through with a knife through your throat."

"Works for me. Just know you can't rush good soup." She folded her arms. "You get me what I need, and you'll have the best cauldron of soup you ever tasted."

A VERY SPECIAL RECIPE

For half a breath, Erryn thought Ilvan might change his mind and tell her to get up those stairs before he dragged her.

Then he blinked and called out over his shoulder, "Thurra, Nendri, start preparing a fire up there. You." He pointed at Erryn. "Tell us what ingredients you need."

She glanced up into the sky and started counting off on her fingers as if actually trying to remember a recipe rather than running through a list of likely and unlikely ingredients. "Well…rosemary, garlic, yarrow, chives, lamb root, and wolf's bane to start. Turnips and potatoes if you've got them. Carrots are good for the journey."

This would be a fine step of a dance to navigate. The ingredients couldn't be too unlikely for them to find or else they'd give up and go forward with their original plan, but it had to be challenging enough to let her stall until she came up with something better or

Ryul got there. This was a decent start. At least a couple should give them a little pause—wait...

Disa started pulling out several of the ingredients from the bags. Nendri called out that there was lamb root in his, and Alrik said he had more garlic if they needed it. Everything they gathered up was also in large enough quantities it would be difficult to say it wasn't enough.

"Venison and a couple antlers," Erryn said, lifting her shoulders. Antlers shouldn't be so easy—

Disa retrieved antlers from the cave and laid them on the ground next to the potatoes and turnips. "These good enough, dear?"

"Um, yes."

"Good, because the longer we keep working on that portal, the more it scares off everything else. We're gonna have to finish here soon, or else there'll be nothing. What else do you need?"

"Um...I'll also need, um...leeks, onions, parsley, kingsfoil, polka berries, salt, and—" She blinked as Disa and Ilvan were already digging out these items. All right. "Stag moss, silverwood bark, parsnips, parsley, barley, dried eel, red obain."

None of those items tripped them up either. The mound of ingredients became enormous.

"Anything else?" Disa asked.

Erryn pursed her lips. She needed something a little more flexible for her purposes. "Oh!" She snapped her fingers. "Whispering rocks and hag stones."

Bet they didn't just have those lying around in their

travel bags. Especially since there was no such thing as whispering rocks.

"I know where to get those." Disa picked up a walking stick and struck out from the camp.

Erryn refrained from raising an eyebrow. That at least would buy more time and allow her to sort out the rest of the plan. These people were swift workers, but at least they couldn't make water boil faster. Still, if there was anything they could do faster, they seemed determined to get it done.

Nendri went to get the water as Thurra hauled the cauldron up the stairs. She suggested that perhaps she could start chopping the onions and peeling the potatoes. He insisted she do everything on the platform. They would bring her whatever she needed when she needed it. Even though that meant multiple runs with the different ingredients.

Ilvan then pointed to the platform. "Get up there now, or the deal is off."

"Can't I take a little more time to savor the sight of the staircase from down here? I want to commit it to memory."

He glowered at her, then pointed again.

"Fine."

She sighed dramatically and then strode toward the staircase, trying to take her time without looking like that was what she was doing. They still had a couple hours to go before sunset. From there, Ryul would have to figure out where she was. Buttons might help him. Ryul insisted he wasn't a good protector or tracking dog, but she knew that little dog could find her anywhere.

As she set her foot on the first of the mossy stairs, the air changed. It hummed and buzzed, trying to pull her into a haze. Even without the portal active at the top, it was still alive. In its own way. Maybe a little angry too about being forced to stay here.

"I don't mean you any harm," she whispered, unsure if that would do any good. "I don't want to make soup on you, but they said I have to, so I suppose I do."

The haze lessened a little, but it still buzzed in her ears.

Up, up, she climbed until she reached the top. She was only about twenty feet in the air, but it felt as if she had climbed much longer. The broken platform at the top was large enough for the fire, a log to sit on, and another upturned log to chop on. If the portal itself arrived, the platform would expand. At least it had when she had walked up the last one. It had been rather mesmerizing. As if it was calling to her. This one probably just wanted her to leave.

Sitting down on the log, she stared into the flames. Already, tiny bubbles formed in the cauldron as the water heated. Traelan sitting below on the camp side meant she couldn't even use this as a weapon. The dull knife they provided her for peeling and chopping wasn't going to be much good, although...

"I need one more thing," she called down.

"What could you possibly need?" Ilvan demanded.

"A frying pan and some bacon, please. The magic in

the stairs feels upset, and bacon will calm it right down."

"We've got fatback," Ilvan responded dryly.

"That'll work! And go ahead and bring up the onions and leeks. I'm going to get this started." She rubbed her hands together briskly. All she needed was time and wit.

Nendri brought her what she requested. After she thanked him, she organized herself. The fire crackled and popped, warming her face and making her sweat. She tore some strips from her skirt and wrapped them around her hands so she wouldn't burn herself if she had to grab the skillet quickly.

This might actually work.

She peeled, chopped, and diced. As the water came to a boil, she added the ingredients in with care and precision as if every step of the process was a work of art.

Disa trotted back into camp, face flushed. She held up two grey sacks of clacking rocks. "I have them!"

"What?" Erryn nearly dropped the little knife. How had she gotten whispering rocks? She'd just made those up.

Disa handed her the two cloth bags. The smaller one with a red ribbon held the hag stones. Perfectly ordinary as best she could tell. The other held polished grey-blue stones that—she drew one out, aware of an eerie whisper rising from the bag. Were they actually whispering?

She frowned. "Wonderful. This looks perfect."

She leaned closer. Were they actually talking?

"Oh, look at my friend," Traelan shouted from below. "How funny she is! Pretending she doesn't know better than to listen to the curses and words of doom from the whispering stones. Very funny indeed. Now, stop joking and finish that soup. If this works, they've promised to let both of us go back to our very quiet lives."

"You heard him." Ilvan gave her a hard stare from below. "This is taking too long."

Disa sighed. "I'm afraid it is. You'll have to hurry, dear. We really can't waste much more time on this."

"This gets done when it gets done." Shaken, Erryn tightened the string and tucked the bags in her pocket. A cold unease passed over her. "Those go in later anyway—unless they talk me out of it. Thank you for getting them."

Ilvan did not laugh. Neither did any of the others.

Everyone was getting impatient. And she still needed time.

She continued with her tasks, making herself look as occupied and mystical as she could manage. Either Nendri or Thurra stayed on the other side of the fire, watching her as she tended to her tasks. Neither engaged in much conversation, and too many attempts to talk resulted in Ilvan threatening her once more.

Soon, the sun set.

Ilvan demanded an update. She assured him that she was working as swiftly as she could, but it wasn't ready just yet. The ingredients needed to meld more.

The minutes ticked by. The sky darkened.

Her skin prickled with anticipation, and the back of

her neck tightened. With all the rest of the vegetables sliced and now in the cauldron, she sliced the fatback thin and fried up small strips. The cast iron skillet sat directly on the coals, heating up thoroughly as it accumulated more and more grease.

How much longer could she drag this out?

The burning logs shifted, cracking apart. Sparks rose, the coals glowing deep red as the wood charred soot-black and ash-white.

Ilvan strode to the side of the staircase next to Traelan. He set his hands on his ragged leather belt, both ominously near the swords sheathed on either side. "This is taking too long," he growled.

"You can't rush magical soup, all right?" She shrugged dramatically. "You've waited this long. You can wait a little longer."

"Portals are weakest in the hours before dawn. We are dangerously close now."

"Then let me finish preparing the soup, and we can open the portal tomorrow. Problem solved!" She lifted the spoon in the air to underscore her point.

"No." Ilvan turned to Disa. "You have all the ingredients she used?"

"Memorized." Disa tapped one tattooed finger to her temple. "Just a matter of proportions and time. We could probably get it with time, and we can keep the fire going with what's up there in case it does just need time." Her expression grew grimmer. "But time is the one thing we're running low on."

Oh. Erryn blinked. Polph. Telling them the ingredients had been a mistake. She shouldn't have said that was all.

"The soup isn't done, and you're breaking our agreement." She squared her shoulders, attempting to make herself as imposing as possible.

"You didn't deliver, human. Prepare to put her through, Thurra. Nendri, help her if the girl fights back," Ilvan called up. "Alrik, cut the kytobar."

"Just give the woman more time," Traelan snapped. "You say you have shown me the proper respect, but you aren't willing to grant a full night and day to see if something can be done to permanently—" He shouted with pain as Alrik cut his arms and palms. Black blood flowed out of the wounds.

Thurra unsheathed her carved short sword. "Don't make this harder than it has to be," she said grimly. "None of us like this."

"Then don't do it." Erryn crouched down, her hand near the cast iron skillet. "I'd rather not hurt you, but I will."

"You? Hurt me? What? Are you gonna try to fry me?" She strode around the fire.

Erryn sprang up and struck Thurra in the shoulder with the cast iron skillet, spilling hot grease on her arm and knocking her off the staircase. The woman fell into the leaves below with a shriek of pain and surprise.

Something hissed and sparked at the edge of the platform. The rocks extended outward. A glowing red-purple lined portal appeared, shimmering and glowing in the darkness. It hummed louder and sharper, like a whole hive of bees. If she moved back even a half step, she'd risk falling through.

Footsteps pounded toward her. She spun back around.

Nendri charged up the stairs, short sword ready, eyes blazing.

Erryn lifted the skillet like it was a club. "You want some of the same?" she shouted at him.

A sharp little bark rang out into the night. Not from the ground, but up in the trees. In the air!

The fir branches snapped out of the way as Buttons flew out, barking and growling. Her mouth fell open as she gasped in delight. He was flying! The little pup had his paws splayed out like he wasn't even sure how he was doing this, and his little tail lashed back like a whip, but he was flying.

Nendri gaped at him, eyes bugging. "What in the—"

Buttons slammed into his face, snarling and biting.

Nendri screeched and fell back. His foot tipped over the edge of the staircase, and he crashed backward. Buttons pulled up just in time to break free and flew toward Erryn, barking and wagging his tail as if to ask if he had done well.

"Oh, sweet baby!" She swept Buttons up in one arm and kissed him between the eyes. "You tracked me down, and you found me. And you flew!"

Buttons barked. His stubby tail struck her arm.

"This means you're just as good as a garm, doesn't it? Better even!"

"Erryn!" Traelan shouted.

She froze as she glimpsed movement below. Ilvan

had a crossbow pointed at her. She tightened her grip on the frying pan. Guess she'd find out if she could use it as a shield.

"Walk through the portal now," he growled. "And you can take your little dog if you like."

A purple shadow shot down and struck the ground next to the firepit. The earth cracked under his feet. Sparks rose from the fire.

Ryul?

He stood, his stance broad as his wings flared and his arms spread, making himself look even larger than he had in the cottage. His eyes glowed with red-purple fury as he bared his fangs.

"Which of you stole my woman?" he snarled.

Well, that made her feel a way. Polph, ordinarily she didn't like being called "woman," but putting "my" in front of it and having him be the one to say it, and she was ready to jump him from here.

Ilvan swung around to face Ryul, his finger starting to tighten on the trigger. Ryul glared at him and curled two fingers in. Ilvan's eyes bulged as he started to lift up into the air.

Alrik crouched down, his gaze fixed on Ryul, blade at the ready. He started forward. Ryul curled two more fingers, and Alrik lurched up into the air, gagging.

"Do none of you understand what you are dealing with? Have none of you battled a blood fae before? I could rip the blood out of your veins and turn it into ropes to bind you before any of you could reach me."

Disa darted toward him, a dagger flashing in her hand.

Ryul barely glanced in her direction as he curled another two fingers in. She skidded backward and rose into the air. "A half-skilled blood fae could make all of you dance like marionettes."

He twisted his hand around, flexing his fingers and then snapping them against his palms. Thurra and Nendri shot up into the air as well, twitching and flailing.

Erryn drew back, holding Buttons close but keeping his face turned from the fight. Was he going to kill them?

He flung all five onto the far side of the clearing beyond the staircase. They skidded across the stony soil, raking over the pine needles and low shrubs. For half a breath, they lay there motionless, groaning. Ilvan started to struggle up. Disa grabbed for his arm, and he collapsed.

"I could stop the blood beating through all of your hearts," Ryul snarled, striding toward them. His dragon-like wings were almost fully visible now, catching the firelight and burning with deepening light through translucent veins and bones. "Consider this your first and only warning. If you ever attempt this portal debauchery again or harm even one hair on my woman's head, your blood will turn to ash in your veins. Now, go!"

Coughing and gasping, the five staggered to their feet. Nendri limped along between Ilvan and Disa while Alrik helped Thurra up. Within seconds, they disappeared into the forest, and the night swallowed them up.

Ryul turned, his wings surging with color and then collapsing inward. "Did they hurt you?" He started up the stairs before she could answer.

"No, I'm fine." She let Buttons down, then straightened, intending to go down to him.

Oh!

He snatched her up, his arms snapping tight around her as he held her close and kissed her cheeks and her lips in rapid succession. "You're certain? You're all right?"

"Yes," she gasped.

She returned his kisses, almost frantic with need. His lips were so firm and yet soft against hers, sending warmth cascading through her body.

Tears spilled down her cheeks. "Ryul, I'm so sorry. I panicked. It wasn't you, I swear—"

"No, I'm sorry. Quinn was wrong. I didn't know they would do that. They should never have said those things."

"But Quinn was right. You shouldn't have to suffer like that for me. It's wrong, and I never meant to—"

"Pardon me," Traelan called out from the stone slab below. "Could this conversation wait another few seconds and one of you assist me in getting a hand free? I can tend to the rest on my own, but that will be a touch more difficult if I bleed out."

She broke free from the kiss, horrified. That was right. He was bleeding out!

"I forgot. I'm coming, Traelan."

"No need to rush," Traelan responded. "I won't die

in the next thirty seconds unless something dreadful happens."

She hurried down the staircase with Buttons trailing along behind and Ryul moving with even slower deliberation as if he was taking in everything about what had happened.

"No curse on them if they should harm a hair on my head?" Traelan said, looking to Ryul.

"You're a kytobar. None of that hair is yours." Ryul offered a small smile. "The only thing real about you is your blood and your voice. And apparently your peril at the moment."

Erryn halted as she reached Traelan. The red-orange light framed him with horrifying vividness. He'd never looked so dreadful. His face was blotched with red marks while other triangular sections were either livid white or pale green. His hands had turned white, and the scars on them had gone green-black. She picked up Alrik's fallen dagger and cut his hands free.

Traelan winced. "And my feelings. Let's not forget about those."

She pulled the strips of cloth from her hands to wrap around his. "You've lost a lot of blood, Traelan. They cut you deep. Let's get you bound up."

Traelan shook his head. "I'll close it. It'll be fine. Just couldn't have bled out much more."

She cut through the rest of the ropes as Ryul came alongside them.

"They were collecting your blood," he said. "Has your blood been altered? Have they drugged you?"

"No. It's fresh from the river," Traelan replied with a dry smile. He placed his hand over one of the long open cuts. "Fortunately, my currents move slow."

"Then hold still."

Ryul traced a pattern in the air, gaze turned down on the blood in the vessel and the grooves of the stone slab. The blood became like a sleek black ribbon and rose into the air. He twitched his index finger, then rolled it, forming a long looping oval shape. The ribbon of blood followed the path, shimmering and twisting in the moonlight until it dove into the wound.

Traelan flinched.

Erryn raised an eyebrow. That actually was impressive.

"You have quite a lot of mastery for one your age," Traelan said.

Ryul scoffed, but the hint of a pleased smile formed on his lips as he continued tracing the air with his finger in long even swoops. "When one's family departs the traditional paths, rigorous training is required of everyone."

Traelan nodded, then shuddered. "Too bad you can't warm it back up before you put it back in."

"Stop complaining," Erryn said, striking his shoulder lightly. "You'll heal faster now."

Hopefully. That was how it worked, wasn't it?

"It's like having dozens of ice serpents shooting up your veins but without the exhilarating high afterward," Traelan responded. He blew out a long breath as the last of the blood wove into his vein. Gritting his teeth, he clamped his hand over one wound, then the next. "Not that either of you should try that." He shook his head as he healed his other arm next. "My thanks, young blood fae. This does speed up my recovery greatly." He pulled the charms off and held his hands to his face. Steam rose from between his fingers as he breathed out heavily. "Oh, those wretched amateurs." He then threaded his hands through his hair and straightened. "A shame you dealt with them before I could contribute."

"Would your method have involved eating them?" Ryul reached for Erryn's hand and guided her back away from Traelan.

"It is an effective method," Traelan responded. "No one comes back from it."

"You said you don't eat humans." Erryn scowled, uncomfortable at that thought.

"I said I wouldn't harm *you*." He flashed her a toothy smile before returning his focus to Ryul. "Not that I would dare lay a claw or scale on the beloved of such an abnormally advanced blood fae. Assuming none of what we witnessed tonight was smoke and mirrors. Not that I would expect you to admit it. It was impressive regardless." He staggered to his feet, adjusted his hat, and smoothed out the long pheasant feather. "As you both can handle matters on your own, I will presume you would like to be left to your own devices. My thanks to you both." He bowed at the waist and gave a flourish. "Good night, dear friends."

THE PARTING OF WAYS

"So…" Erryn turned toward Ryul after Traelan disappeared. She angled her chin up as she gave him a playful side eye. "I'm your woman?"

A smile twitched at his lips, but then his expression turned stoic as he studied her. His half-shaded gaze traveled up and down her body. "I'd rather you not be anyone else's, so yes."

"Is it just my soup-making abilities you want me for?"

"I feel like what I want is obvious."

Buttons barked and hopped up on his hind legs, pawing at her knee.

"Buttons did well tonight. You didn't see him, but he was every bit as good as a garm."

His eyebrow arched. "You've never actually seen a garm fight, have you?"

She scooped the dog up and held him out to Ryul. "He did so good. Kiss him and tell him you're proud of him."

He scratched Button's tummy. "Proud of you." His smile went crooked. Then he sighed. "You did good, you ugly little dog."

Buttons panted, flailed his little limbs, and fluttered his wings. She kissed him on the top of the head and set him down once again.

"He flew right at that one man's face and bit him on the nose and pushed him off the staircase. And he was so cute! His legs were like this." She demonstrated, stiffening her arms and legs. Then, darting forward, she swept up against him and kissed him on the lips. "And you were incredible."

"So were you. You're sure they didn't hurt you?"

"The most they did was when they knocked me out. Someone hit me in the back of the head."

"Let me see."

"It's nothing—"

He had already moved behind her and lifted her hair. Small prickles of pleasure swept down her neck as his fingers grazed the delicate skin there.

"There's a decent bruise here. And a little swelling. I could try to help it heal faster, but head wounds are a little riskier."

"It'll heal. I've had worse." Especially when she had traveled on her own. "And considering what could have happened, I'm grateful that this is all that there was. I just want you to know…I wasn't running because of you."

"I know. I talked with Quinn. They were completely wrong, and I am so sorry."

"I panicked. It was like everything was closing in on

me, and it was so loud. I couldn't take it. I had to get away. It reminded me—" Her voice broke. The memories started rising again.

He stroked her cheek. "You don't have to explain. I understand. That wasn't how I wanted it to go."

"I know. But Quinn is right. You shouldn't have to suffer because of me. And that prism—"

"That prism is the only way I know how to protect you from the wish."

"Maybe that isn't something you can protect me from. Maybe that is part of what it means to be in a relationship with you." Her heart started to beat faster, her palms sweating. Her posture tightened. "Maybe that is something you can't fix."

"I can, though, if you'll just let me. What's one more curse? I've already got several." He spread his arms wide. "I can take another one, especially if it means I get to be with you."

"One more curse is a lot. Any curse is a lot."

"Maybe on a human," he said. "On a blood fae, not the same."

"Doesn't mean it isn't a problem. And the phrasing on that prism is disturbingly open-ended. You should probably destroy it as soon as you're able. Can you imagine what would happen if that got into the hands of the wrong person?"

"Well—" He scratched his head, then took her arm in his as he contemplated this. "That would be bad. But isn't that all the more reason you should use it?"

"No! Can it be destroyed?"

"Yes."

"Then it needs to be destroyed."

"But if I destroy it, you can't use it."

"That would be the general idea. You've got a random charm bouncing in your pocket that would let someone bind whatever they wanted and give you the consequences."

He continued to try to persuade her as they walked through the forest. As before, he guided her and moved branches out of the way while she carried Buttons. The damp scent of wet earth and leaf mold grew stronger as they moved away from the fire and the camp. The moon was full, the trees weren't so close together, and it was far easier to see.

"If I could think of another solution, I would offer it," he said. "Otherwise, wouldn't our living together simply be putting you at risk? Especially if—well—I think I could do good things to you that would make you want to say you love me. Maybe scream it."

Her cheeks heating, she shook her head. "That's—you're getting me flustered. You're right. It's hard not say it even now. Hard to not even think about it too. And I'm afraid of what will happen, but my gut says that using that prism is wrong."

"So we'll just be careful then? What if you slip? I don't want you to feel trapped."

"Have you given thought to what you would wish for?"

"Yes. And I'll continue to. If you ever feel like you can say those words and offer that wish, I will do all within my power to make it good and beautiful, and I won't give in to any temptation with it."

His fingers tightened around her hand. The moonlight that filtered through the canopy here was just enough that she could see his face. It highlighted the planes and lines of his jaw and cheeks.

"You're a good fae, Ryul."

He shook his head, his long lavender hair brushing his shoulders with the movement. A few strands caught on an errant branch. "Not a good blood fae, though. At least not from what I've heard about my kind."

"A fae man I—"

She stopped herself. It really was so easy, and those three words practically begged to be spoken now.

He smiled as if he understood. "My family will like you too. I have no doubt of that."

"You mean like Quinn does?"

He laughed wryly and drew her to the right. "There's a thornbush there."

They carried on for the rest of the night, picking a path through the moonlight and darkness, moving beneath broad branches and climbing over rotted logs. Nothing disturbed them. It was as if the moonlight-dappled forest had been reserved for them and them alone. He kept his arm around her waist most of the time, and more than once, they lapsed into pleasant silence. He was someone she just enjoyed being with. Even when words weren't enough.

At last, they stopped at a point where the trees fell back. Dull purple mushrooms with pale stalks clustered around the overgrown roots of a grey-barked elm. Moss clung to the cracked stones, and the tree branches parted to allow a full view of the sky.

He laced his fingers together and placed them on the top of his head, sighing. "I'm sorry, Erryn. I can't get us back to the castle or to the boundary marker before dawn breaks."

She set Buttons down and peered up into the sky. The rich indigo had already lightened to a softer purple, and the lavender and yellow of dawn spread across the eastern sky. Based on how long it had taken him to reach her, she guessed the castle was quite a far distance still. She had no real idea where they were.

"If you go ahead on your own, can you make it? Fly with all your strength and speed. I'll be fine here. I'll get somewhere safe. With that staircase in the air and what Ilvan and his band were doing, most of the predators are gone. Maybe all of them. That's where the night gryphons went, I think, so you can go on ahead."

His grimace turned into a sad smile as he leaned forward and kissed her forehead. "Are you trying to torment me? You want me to spend even a minute more away from you?"

"I don't want you to be hurt."

"I suppose we shouldn't have been born then. Life is full of pain." He hugged her close, burying his face in her hair. "The castle is east of here. The boundary marker is south. It'll be the easiest one to find. Now, I know you don't want it, Erryn, but please, think about what I've said. If you're willing to accept me, I will return that prism to you, and we can bind those words from your mouth. I don't need you to say them. All I want from you is you. For my part, I will do whatever it takes to be with you, Erryn. But what I want most is for you to be happy. If you cannot be happy with me, I will accept that. If you can, just tell me what I must do. Use the prism. I will take whatever it brings. I swear to you that I will not regret it."

"You seem to have a hard time understanding this, so I'll be clearer. It will wound you, Ryul. Do you think I could put that on you?"

"Does it count as wounding me if it frees you from torment?" He clasped her hands between his and kissed her fingertips. "I do not count it as such."

Off in the distance, morning larks called out the first notes of dawn's arrival. His shoulders sagged.

She slid her hand along his strong jaw and up along his cheekbones. "How can I make this easier?"

The smile that reached his lips warmed her heart as he pulled her closer. "Stay with me until the dawn takes me. Be with me. Let me hold you. Just let us be."

She twined her arms around him and rested her ear just above his heart. "I can do that."

The day would not pass swiftly enough before they were reunited. Emotion choked her. There was so much she wanted to tell him, but the words stuck in her throat. Not just the three that would change everything, but so much more.

The birds sang louder now. Little chirping songs that told one another "I'm here. I made it through another night."

She pressed her face into his chest. She'd be singing something similar when night fell.

He winced, but then he curled closer to her. One

hand cradled the back of her head above the bruise while the other pressed against her back.

It was starting.

She held him tighter but tilted her face up to look into his beautiful amethyst eyes with flecks of indigo and black. "I'll see you soon."

"Not nearly soon enough," he whispered.

The soft rays of light passed over them. His body tensed against hers. She wanted to clutch him even closer, but she peered up at him instead.

"I—" She bit the words back before they escaped. "I can't wait to kiss you again."

He winced a little but smiled, then opened his mouth to speak. Before he could, he vanished like smoke on the sunbeams.

She shuddered, suppressing a cry. It was only for a little while. Only for a day. Her heart swelled and ached. She couldn't have felt more for him if she had tried.

Pressing her hand over her heart, she steadied herself and her breaths. Oh, those three words did burn within her. And they were true. So true. There could never be another like him. How could she still have any fear about this?

"Pining for him already?" a familiar voice asked.

She hinged her gaze to the right, not sure if she was surprised to see Traelan there or not. What was surprising, though, was that his clothing was once again immaculate, and his wounds had all been healed. He looked every bit as sharp and dashing as the day she had met him.

"Were you waiting for him to leave?"

Buttons barked and trotted up to him, sniffing the air. His tail wagged as if he was happy to see the kytobar. She still wasn't sure whether she trusted the little dog's judgment.

"Not precisely. I suppose you could view it that way but not for anything untoward. I needed to get those stakes up from the staircase. Then I heard your voice in the distance and thought why not finish our conversation."

"I wasn't aware we were in the middle of one." She looked him up and down as she set her hands on her sash. "You just so happened to have a change of clothes out in the forest and got yourself all back to your normal state, huh?"

His smile broadened. "It's all an illusion, my dear, but even illusions need restoration. And, yes, we've been in the middle of a conversation for a while now. He's proposed that you reconsider using that cursed prism with the unknown consequences that will only affect him. For what my opinion is worth, I agree with you. Magic isn't something you should try to trick. That only makes it more complicated and more uncomfortable for everyone."

She wrapped her arms around herself tight. "Whoever made this law—whoever stitched it into our souls and seared it into our blood—should be made to pay."

If it weren't for the wish, she'd have jumped Ryul already. There was no way she could have sex with him and not at some point scream how much she loved him.

He shrugged. "Maybe so, but acting foolishly with it won't make it better. It can only make it worse. Magic has many types and many forms. Each one must be respected and understood, regardless of your feelings for it."

"That means my only real choice is to grant the wish or to go back to the soup cottage. I wish I wasn't still scared. I've never met anyone like him. He is kind and thoughtful. He sees tasks that need to be done, and he tries to do them. Even chores that most men don't see."

"Bargains and wishes should never be entered into or granted casually. Perhaps the fear is not a bad thing. There are no real assurances, but there are sometimes exceptions."

She shrugged. There were, and she had already made one for him.

"I will say one more thing." Traelan adjusted his hat. The long pheasant feathers gleamed in the morning light. "You don't have to choose between going back to that little soup cottage or sticking with the blood fae. I like your nerve and grit. You know your way around a frying pan in more ways than one, and your soup is rather good. If you'd like to join me, I could certainly use someone to assist me in my travels and studies. And I stand by my promise not to harm you."

Buttons barked in response, head cocked as if that was ridiculous.

It was.

She laughed. "What?"

"It's a great big world out there. Those aren't your

only two choices. He said he wants you to be happy. You could go off and make your own way for a time and then return when you're ready to make that bargain. If you want to. You could change your mind any time. And the space away from him would help you avoid tripping into that bargain unintentionally."

He was right. That was a possibility.

She straightened, finding it easier to breathe after the laughter. "I appreciate the offer. I know what I want, though."

He chuckled. "Well, the pleasure has certainly been all mine. Ryul is a lucky fellow. You're a rather useful companion."

Something in the way he said it made her draw back. He hadn't meant it. The offer. Not the well wishes. If she had said yes, he would have lost respect for her.

She tilted her head, her focus narrowing in on him. "What's your game, kytobar?"

"Game?" he asked with over-exaggerated innocence. His eyes widened until the whites were visible all around his bright-green irises as he pressed his hand to his chest. "No game at all. Just an awareness that the choice between an over-crowded soup cottage and what amounts to an essentially haunted castle with a handsome blood fae might make one think that there weren't any real choices in the matter."

"And if I had said yes?"

"We'd have had a good time, but you would never have said yes. I know that look, and it warms what little remains of my cold dead heart. Offering you a choice just made you realize what you wanted. And I hope that all goes well for you." He bowed his head, closing his eyes. "May all your paths be blessed, the wind always at your back, and your purse always full."

With that, he winked, turned, and strode away until he disappeared over a hill farther into the forest.

Buttons barked again, then looked up at her.

"Yes, I know," she said. "Come on. Let's go."

She snapped her fingers and then dropped her hand to her pocket. Her eyes widened. That kytobar had just stolen those whispering rocks. How had he even gotten close enough? He hadn't touched her, had he?

Scoffing, she shook her head. Well, that figured, but maybe he was right about the rest of what he'd said.

Buttons circled in front of her, barking another question.

"No," she said. "I'm not going after him for that. We have somewhere else we need to be, and it's going to take us a bit to get there."

She started toward the floating castle then, contemplating all that had happened. It was far easier to find her way there in daylight than it was at night, mostly because she could see the castle through the branches. Even when the foliage became too thick, a few steps farther and it came into view once more.

Her stomach tightened as she drew closer. Despite Ryul's assurances, she suspected Quinn still wouldn't be happy. And she needed Quinn to at least accept her presence for a little bit if she was going to make this work.

She stepped out into the clearing. The grass seemed

shorter and crunchier now, the leaves on the surrounding trees more yellow and red. It was as if the season was changing faster here. It still smelled like stone and woodsmoke, though.

"Hello, Quinn," she said, setting her hands on her waist. "I need you to listen to me, and when you respond, I really need you to not yell or raise your voice, if you'd be so kind."

The stones creaked as if in response. The glossy doors seemed to glower at her from their great height.

Buttons barked up at it as well.

"Now, I know you care about Ryul, and I certainly don't blame you for that. He is one of the best people I have ever known of any race. And while he and I did not start off on the right foot, I assure you that now—if anything were about to happen to him—I would happily club the threat with a skillet."

More stones creaked. An odd sound huffed out. Was that a laugh?

She broadened her stance. "I'd do better than that, too, if I could, but I am just a human. So all my violence requires creativity. I don't have magic. And I know you might not like me, but you and I need to get to the bottom of this because I've made up my mind what I want, and I'd like to tell Ryul in person. So you're going to need to help me with that. Please?"

The wind stirred through the stones, sighing and whispering.

She remained where she was, listening. If it took all day, that was fine. She knew exactly what she needed to do.

RYUL

Ryul dragged himself up out of the narrow stone chamber, grimacing. It never hurt any less to be ripped apart like that and cast into darkness in whatever this dank place was. To his knowledge, the curse didn't throw him into a real part of the castle. Rather it was some place in between. Some sort of magical void.

"Are you all right, Ryul?" Quinn asked, their voice wavering with emotion. "You should rest. At least for a little bit."

"This is all your fault, you bloated ball of consciousness," he grumbled, glaring up at the ceiling, even though he wasn't sure if that was where Quinn was at the moment. "If you'd listened to me from the start, this never would have happened."

"Hmmm." Quinn did not sound convinced.

Ryul collapsed on the stone, rolled into a seated position, and held his head. He ached, and the cold here bit all the way through his bones. Here, loneliness and isolation were most vividly epitomized. His own breaths echoed as loudly as if there was someone else nearby. But there wasn't anyone else near.

There might never be anyone near here ever again.

He and Erryn still needed to talk. And he had to make sure he listened. This wasn't the time to bargain. Even though he desperately wanted to just ask her what it would take. He'd give her anything—anything at all—if she would just agree to stay with him—to be with him.

He closed his eyes, the aching intensifying. It had been worth it to get cast back down into that horrid place and have to make the long grinding crawl back up just to be near her and to feel the warmth of her body against his for those extra moments. Even now, the memory of her smiling at him, her brow slightly twisted with concern and hazel-brown eyes wide, was enough of a consolation. She never had to know how much it hurt to be ripped to shreds and then reformed. She never had to know because she would never understand how much comfort and joy she brought him and how all of that made this worth it.

He drew in a long ragged breath, filling his chest with the damp air.

Tonight though—tonight they would talk. He hoped she would take the prism. After all she had lost, could she possibly say yes to him otherwise?

He couldn't imagine being in her shoes.

The loss of his family had nearly destroyed him. How long had he wailed and attacked the walls and desperately searched for them before realizing there was precious little he could do? But he had never carried the burden of believing it was his fault that they had been separated from him.

Creator help him, he missed her already.

He made his way up the long cracked staircase to his own quarters. Or what had become his quarters. His old bedroom had been lost along with many other rooms that were quite valuable, including the kitchen and the sunroom and the training room. The magic in the castle hadn't adapted to creating new rooms or new items beyond the initial instructions poured into it at its creation. So it carried on as it always did, restocking the larder, eliminating dust, starting fires in the chosen fireplaces, filling pitchers and inkwells, and just generally struggling to function. Not even Quinn could reason with or alter the magic instilled in this place. More than once, it had gotten things wrong, but it did its best, and he appreciated it.

He'd turned the small cartography study into his bedroom. All the remaining rooms were far too large and made him feel tiny and alone. As a child, he had never gone in here, mostly because it had been locked up. None of his siblings or cousins went in either, but that also meant it wasn't drenched in memories that cut him through the heart. It smelled of old cedar, bitter ink, sifting ash, and nova musk. Dried leaves had been pressed between pieces of glass and hung on the wall between framed maps, little notations marked alongside each.

He'd shoved the desk to the far wall and made a bed of what was currently furs and a couple tablecloths topped with two blue blankets. Over the months, he'd tried out different things to make it more comfortable. He had enough to make a separate bed for Erryn if she wanted it, either in here or in one of the other small rooms. Though—admittedly—he hoped she'd be willing to share his if she agreed to stay. It would also be easier because the castle's magic hated change so much that it had taken weeks and weeks to keep it from disassembling his bed and putting the pieces back where they originally belonged.

The fire flared up in the hearth, bright yellow flames that soon dulled to orange. He picked up the cracked porcelain pitcher and poured the cool water into the basin.

However long it took, it didn't matter. As much as a part of him longed to hear her say she loved him—as much as he needed it—he would never force her to say that. It was enough to know that she felt it. He wished she didn't even feel like she needed to.

The air hummed above him as Quinn arrived.

Quinn spoke again, a little louder this time. "You should go reflect in the ballroom."

He scoffed as he scooped up the water and splashed it on his face. Ordinarily, Quinn didn't come into his room, but that meant they were probably even more concerned than usual.

"There's no time for reflection. I know you don't like her, but that doesn't matter. She is the most incredible woman I have ever met. And if you can't appreciate her—well, I don't know what the solution will be, but I doubt you'll like it."

The dull aching of his muscles and marrow was starting to subside. Every time he defied the curse and stayed out in the daylight outside his castle, it hurt more and longer. But there had to be a limit.

"We're certain she has her good traits. But you should not be worried about her. Perhaps she found the kytobar again. He might help her."

Grunting, he splashed more water on his face. He wasn't sure if he trusted that kytobar. Their first meeting had left him uneasy, as if Traelan could see straight through him and all of his tricks. Now that Ryul knew what he was—he suppressed a shudder.

The kytobar hadn't missed a trick. He'd probably picked up on every bluff Ryul had made against those five barbarians. Not that it felt as if he intended to do anything nefarious with it. It was just—uncomfortable. A bluff only had value if it was believable. Those five hadn't known he was at his limits, but that kytobar had. No matter how he had pretended that he could have done more, he had been pressed well to his limit.

His mood worsening, he picked up the towel and dried his face. He hoped Traelan had stayed away from Erryn. On top of everything, he didn't like the way he looked at her. Despite what he promised, he probably did want to eat her. Metaphorically or whatever kytobars did when they actually wanted someone romantically.

"You can't leave the castle until the daylight departs," Quinn pointed out. "So go to the ballroom and watch the sun set. You've spent almost all day trying to get out of that pit. The least you can do is give yourself some calm. It's a noteworthy point. You may find it instructive."

"Instructive how?"

He needed to get ready to find Erryn. As long as she had Buttons, though, he could find her. Eventually. As long as he got properly focused.

"Just go." Quinn's words buzzed in his ears. A sure sign they were annoyed.

The study door slammed open and struck the wall. Other doors slammed open as well.

Cantankerous consciousness.

They were probably right, though. He was just going to brood in here. The fresh air might clear his head and push out all the fears that his family wasn't looking for him anymore and that he'd never find them and that Erryn would leave too. Even if all of that was true, there was nothing he could do at the moment.

He stepped out into the ballroom. Like a couple of the other rooms, large portions of the walls had disintegrated, leaving little more than rubble here. The magic, of course, tried to tidy it as well, clearing away dust and debris as well as weeds. For some reason, it allowed the moss along the very edges to grow and trail down like streamers. Maybe it thought that was beautiful?

The blue-grey marble floor shone like a fractured mirror with all the cuts and cracks marring its smoothness. Most of the carved columns had vanished. Perhaps they floated around someone else's castle now, or perhaps they'd fallen away.

But it was beautiful in a broken, distorted way.

The sun had not yet disappeared beyond the horizon. Its vibrant light turned the sky a myriad of shades with the deep purple-black of night creeping ever closer from the east.

He missed stretching out on the grass and watching clouds and drifting off to sleep. Just like he missed a lot of things. It probably wouldn't be as enjoyable to do alone.

The wind changed directions, blowing against the back of his head and ruffling his hair. He paused, noting a different but familiar scent. How—

He turned his head, then froze, his heart clenching tight.

Erryn stood at the top of the fractured staircase, her shoulders lifted and her face flushed. She wore an elegant rose-pink gown with a long train that trailed across the stones. The little silver belt had tiny leaves. It set off her auburn-red hair. Her hair wasn't pulled back in that lopsided bun or tied back with a ribbon any longer. She'd combed and styled it so that it flowed over her back with a little gathered up and clipped with a silver-leafed rose barrette

Tiny pearls and rosebuds lined the dress's hem, and the angel sleeves had a little coil of shirring just above the elbow and thin bands of silver-white ribbon.. Every facet of it set off her body to its full advantage.

If this was the dress she'd said was a mistake, she couldn't be more wrong. Utterly impractical and perfectly stunning. His chest tightened as the blood surged faster through his veins. How was it possible for her to be even more beautiful than before?

"I hope you don't mind," she said. "Quinn and I had a bit of a talk. I think we're in agreement now. In fact, they're keeping an eye on Buttons for me."

"Oh?" He started toward her. It felt as if he was in a dream. Was it possible he was dreaming?

She halted in front of him, just out of his reach. "I've been thinking. I am older than you. And wiser."

"Such an old woman." He smiled but did not close the distance between them. She could still tell him no. She might be wanting to tell him that wisdom meant they must part forever.

"I have a speech prepared. Don't get me flustered." She ducked her head, her face turning pinker.

No. This wasn't bad news. That was just his fears whispering again.

He nodded and kept his arms at his sides, though he desperately wanted to take hold of her and drown every fear out.

She cleared her throat, her gaze darting back to his once more. "I'm also far more experienced in everything that is not related to being a blood fae or navigating a floating castle or flying. And through my years, I have fallen in love and come to understand what it means to be loved, used, and abused. After wounds, it is always hard to trust again. Experience can be a bitter teacher. And I can't say I am not afraid, Ryul. This might be the scariest thing I've done in my life. But..." She lifted her chin. "I absolutely refuse to bind these words from my lips."

He swallowed hard, his hands clenched at his sides with need.

"So..." She stepped closer. "Ryul, I have something I need to tell you."

He met her gaze. Could he touch her? Would that disturb her now?

Her face had paled, but she nodded as if she read his thoughts. She placed her hand on his chest, spreading her fingers over the thin fabric of his silk shirt. Her touch seared through him, igniting the flames he'd struggled to contain.

He closed the distance between them, bringing one arm around her waist and touching the small of her back. She fit so perfectly in his arms. Even better when he held her tighter.

"Ryul," she said again, her voice trembling. "I love you."

Relief flooded through him—then a sharp surge of energy. Everything went black, the energy coiling and expanding within him, too intense for him to even breathe. It wiped everything away and left him spiraling in darkness.

No one had ever given him the power of a wish before. In all the times he'd heard what it was like—all the times he'd been warned of what the temptation and corruption would feel like—nothing compared to its reality.

It sparked and grew within him, filling his ears and drowning out his other senses like the roar of a tornado. It rooted his muscles into place, twining through him and binding him in chaotic paralysis as if he were nothing except a conduit.

He could choose.

Anything. He could have anything. Ask for anything. And maybe—

An old raw panicked desire rose in his chest as memories peeked up. What did he want most of all? To be home again. To have his family once more. Siblings, cousins, aunts, uncles, parents, and more. Their faces flashed within his mind. All the loss. All the sorrow.

The possibilities cut through his heart and sliced through his mind, pulling him into an even darker place. They whispered in his ears and filled his mind. Everything. It would be all right. What was the harm in asking? Why not? What reason was there to have restraint when this had been given so freely?

The thoughts crushed in around him, driving everything else away.

His arms tightened. Something warm pressed against him. The dullness in his mind fought against recognition. But it was a familiar form.

Erryn!

A panicked jolt shot through him. He focused on her. He was holding her—why did she feel so far away? He had to come back—had to find his way back.

He smelled her hair and that distinct combination of rosemary, celery, and garlic that always clung faintly to her even beneath the fresh scent of soap. He felt her gentle curves and her warmth, and her heartbeat—her heart was racing so fast.

Oh.

A pang of awareness cut even deeper. He was frightening her. How long had he been silent?

The chaotic power of the wish stilled within him.

It was all just temptation. A ruse that tried to contaminate what actually was with the offer of what might be. Seeing it for what it was shriveled that temptation up even as it suggested that perhaps their love was strong enough that all would unite to grant it.

No.

He couldn't risk her. His family and home were gone. One day, perhaps, they would find one another again. But he wouldn't place that burden on her. She meant too much to him. She didn't deserve that burden.

The clamor and humming faded as his sight returned, and he became more aware of her again. What she'd given him was powerful. Beautiful. Freely given. Wholly felt. Precious beyond words. Just like her.

He nuzzled her, bringing his mouth to her ear. All that he had planned was gone, but he knew precisely what to say as clarity returned to his mind and body.

"Erryn, I wish for your happiness, joy, and fulfillment. That we be bound by love, by choice, by blood. My heart to yours. My will with you. My life to its end with you alone. Forever and always. No matter how long or how short, forever my love with you."

A ragged breath followed as she collapsed against his chest. "I love you," she whispered tearfully. "I love you, Ryul. Forever and always."

"And I love you." He wiped the tears from her cheek with his thumb, one at a time. "More than anything."

She laughed. "For a moment there, I was afraid—"

Her voice broke. "I was afraid you—" She ducked her head back to his chest.

"The temptation was there, but I couldn't risk you. I would never risk you." He hugged her close. "No matter what happens, so long as I have you, I can be happy."

He swept his mouth over hers. She pressed up into him, her lips soft and inviting, her body arching against his.

Yes. He'd made the right choice. Happiness flooded him as he lifted her off the ground.

She gasped with laughter and wrapped her arms around his neck. "I'm not going to forget my promise to you either," she said. "We're going to do this together. I'll help you find your family. We'll get your magic back to full strength, and then, we'll find them."

"I might actually believe you," he said.

She kissed his cheek, then nipped at his lower lip. "You should. I know your weakness, and I'll help you find your strength."

He caught her mouth with his, savoring her as he carried her back toward the doorway into the castle. She might not know it yet, but she already had.

AUTHOR'S NOTE

Dear travelers, thank you so much for joining me on this adventure. This was such a fun ride!

Erryn and Ryul's story brought me so much joy, and keeping this in the cozy and warm subgenre of fantasy proved a good welcome challenge. Not that everything went to plan. When Angela Ford and Stephanie BwaBwa first put this set together, I had a particular story in mind.

That is not the story that wound up finished (though I will finish that one eventually).

No, this one cropped up with one scene some time in January. It was relatively simple: Erryn being willing to go toe to toe with a blood fae and clobbering him in the side of the head with a cast iron skillet. After which, she then hogties him and decides to attempt further negotiations after that.

A couple friends found that first snippet hilarious and mentioned Rapunzel from *Tangled*. That made me laugh even more, and the imagery stuck. While this isn't a Rapunzel retelling, I can't help but feel that Erryn would love her and that story. For me, it was a little simpler. I've always had a soft spot for characters with frying pans, starting with Samwise Gamgee (and his "getting the hang of it"). And as someone who has dropped a cast iron skillet on her toe and burned herself on one, I can attest that they are formidable weapons.

Erryn snapped into focus relatively quickly. Her love for Buttons, her tendency to say things she probably shouldn't, and her quick spirit all came together in a cohesive whole. Especially after I attempted some doodles of my own. Her love for Buttons was immediately relatable to me, and I also found myself intrigued by her past, which was a bit of a mystery to me for the first part of the story.

Ryul proved a touch more ambiguous and challenging. In fact, I knew members of his family before I knew him. The whole situation with the separation and his trying to get back has formed the backbone of some other stories in development, and I wasn't expecting him to be the one to show up here in the northern territories. I also didn't expect him to be so good with consent and so mature despite his age. (Some of my characters are significantly older and have a much harder time understanding consent, respect, and support that are rather natural for him.) His initial bluster and harshness comes from a multitude of factors, but the way that he evens out with Erryn warms my heart.

While not much time is spent on the page with the

floating castle, the concept is one I've been playing with for a while. Especially Quinn and Volsrei and others who are like them. Personally, I can't think of anything more terrifying. It has always been a thought that has fascinated me in its various depictions. Howl's Moving Castle and the castle itself in Castlevania don't have consciousnesses per se, but Neil Gaiman's "The Doctor's Wife" as well as horror movies where the house has its own consciousness captured my attention. So now I am finally releasing the stories where I get to explore that concept and put my own twist on it.

Also I've received two questions from early readers consistently that I wanted to make sure I answered here because they're excellent questions.

First, is this part of the TueRahVerse? Yes. This is taking place in one of the Cut Off Worlds that has been transformed significantly and gone through so many changes that they have no real memory of the Tue-Rah (but if you've read through Tue-Rah Chronicles, you know what the purple-red-rimmed portals mean). The races are all (or at least mostly) connected to the original Eight, but they too have undergone significant transformations and specializations.

Whether this will join up with the main Tue-Rah Chronicles Series, I doubt it. I have ideas and plans for where the return of the Tue-Rah and the portals will come into play and how it will affect everything as well as the timeline. But Erryn and Ryul won't be appearing in an epic battle of the Tue-Rah's restoration. My goal with their story and the others within their family is to keep them fairly light (we'll see how well I succeed in that) as well as more accessible.

Erryn and Ryul's story is, however, in the same world as the *Fae Bride Series.* And you'll see references and crossovers from there as the stories continue.

Second, a number of you were concerned about the family situation. Especially Erryn's. So I'll give you a little teensy spoiler. Yes, Erryn believes that her mother and sister are dead (and for good reason). Thus the focus moving forward is mostly on reuniting Ryul with his family. But Erryn's mother and sister will be appearing again as well (in stories with a happy ending). In fact, those of you who participated in the polls and voted on names already helped me pick out their names. And I can't wait to share the details of it all with you. You'll see more in 2024.

Now if you've read this far, I do have a little surprise for you. If you go to https://jmbutlerauthor.com/**bound-by-blood-bonuses/**

This is separate from the preorder bonuses. And the content probably won't be live until June 9. But this is my way of saying an extra big thank you to all of you.

Thank you again for all your support, and please make sure to let me know if you want to read more about Ryul and Erryn.

Much love to you and great joy in all your travels,

Jess

ACKNOWLEDGMENTS

If you've read my acknowledgments in previous stories, you know some of the people I'm going to thank in here, and I will say it again, loud and proud: I couldn't do this without them. And this is probably the first time I have put together a story that all of my loved ones could read without cringing too much or having to close their eyes through some scenes.

First, I owe great thanks to Angela Ford and Stephanie BwaBwa for putting this multi-author series together. This multi-author series was an intriguing one in part because of its subject matter but also because of its limitations. It took me out of my comfort zone in a good way, and I got to create a story that challenged me.

Second, I am so grateful to everyone who helped me make this story better. To Maggie Myers for her edits, Katherine Bennet for her advice on how to simplify and keep it stronger, and Rachel Cass and Nicole Zoltak for their proofreading and commentary. I wouldn't know what to do without them.

Third, I am thankful for my cover designers. Cover Dungeon Rabbit designed both the primary typography cover and did the typography for the underjacket and couple design. Gorgeous work that exceeded my expectations plus so much skill in blending that list of diverse elements I sent her. Natálie Vašutová of Thalia Art designed the underjacket cover with the couple. She captured so much beauty and elegance in that single image that I gasped when I saw it.

Fourth, I am beyond grateful to my friends and family for all of their support through my insanity and writing pursuits. Especially in this one where I regularly bemoaned that I couldn't just have dragons attack to get the plot moving again.

Fifth, I still get good chuckles and much gratitude from all the help my secret reader group members and newsletter subscribers provided in picking out the names for Erryn and Buttons. I have never had so many email responses as I did for Buttons. Not only that, but new names were provided and new ideas as well. I'm going to do a little something special to thank all of you, and if you were participating in the name voting and name ideas, you are incredible. Thank you.

And last but certainly not least, thank you for reading this. Readers like you help make this dream become a reality and encourage authors like me to keep going and keep sharing these stories. I cannot thank you nearly enough. I have some of the absolute best readers in the world, and I am so grateful for you.

ABOUT THE AUTHOR

Jessica M. Butler is an adventurer, author, and attorney who never outgrew her love for telling stories and playing in imaginary worlds. She is the author of the epic fantasy romance series *Tue-Rah Chronicles* including *Identity Revealed, Enemy Known,* and *Princess Reviled, Wilderness Untamed,* and *Shifter Untamed* along with independent stories *Escaping Red Eye, Locked, Cursed,* and *Alone,* set in the same world. She has also written numerous fantasy tales such as *Mermaid Bride, Little Scapegoat, Through the Paintings Dimly, Why Yes, Bluebeard, I'd Love To,* and more. For the most part, she writes speculative fiction with a heavy focus on high fantasy and suspenseful adventures and passionate romances. She lives with her husband and law partner, James Fry, in rural Indiana where they are quite happy with their five cats: Thor, Loptr, Fenrir, Hela, and Herne.

For more books or updates:
www.jmbutlerauthor.com

facebook.com/jmbutler1728
twitter.com/jessicabfry
instagram.com/jessicambutlerauthor

ALSO BY JESSICA M. BUTLER

The Tue-Rah Chronicles

Identity Revealed

Enemy Known

Princess Reviled

Wilderness Untamed

Shifter King

Empire Undone

Tue-Rah Stories

Escaping Red Eye

Locked

Alone

Cursed

Standalones

Slaying the Naga King

The Mermaid Bride

The Celebrity

Little Scapegoat

Vellas

Fae Rose Bride

Anthologies

Of Masks and Magic

Once Upon Now

Vices and Virtues

Fierce Hearts

Adamant Spirits

CPSIA information can be obtained
at www.ICGtesting.com
Printed in the USA
JSHW011116070623
42828JS00004B/128/J